'In a hospital situation, people are different.

'We're geared to treat their illnesses or mend their broken bones, and sexuality seldom interferes with our actions and thoughts.' Laurie smiled, and Samantha felt a laser beam of tension, bright and probing, build up between them. 'Away from the hospital, in the sun and near water, which in itself is aphrodisiac, I see only the beauty, and my mind becomes very unprofessional.'

Dear Reader

When you behave out of character, it is sure to find you out, as Sharon Wirdnam's heroine discovers in SURGEON OF THE HEART. And when trust has been abused, it is hard to accept love again, as Rob finds out in A GENTLE GIANT from Caroline Anderson. We go to Italy in Lisa Cooper's DREAM OF NAPLES, and explore the role of alternative medicine in HAND IN HAND with Margaret Barker. Happy holidays!

The Editor

Lisa Cooper trained as a nurse at a London teaching hospital. After a short spell as a theatre sister, she married an accountant. Her son is a biologist and her daughter is a medical scientist working for sick children. She began to write when she was unable to go back to nursing, and has since had numerous books published.

Recent titles by the same author:

MEDICAL DECISIONS
EASTERN ADVENTURE

DREAM OF NAPLES

BY

LISA COOPER

MILLS & BOON LIMITED
ETON HOUSE   18–24 PARADISE ROAD
RICHMOND   SURREY   TW9 1SR

*First published in Great Britain 1992
by Mills & Boon Limited*

© Lisa Cooper 1992

*Australian copyright 1992
Philippine copyright 1992
This edition 1992*

ISBN 0 263 77815 0

*Set in 10½ on 12 pt Linotron Times
03-9208-52896*

*Typeset in Great Britain by Centracet, Cambridge
Made and printed in Great Britain*

CHAPTER ONE

THE wide but shallow steps swept up to the terrace in front of the cathedral, as if they were hung there like an elaborate tapestry, the variegated stonework stitching a border to the design and merging with the high arches above the terrace. Samantha Croft sank on to a café chair and wondered why there were so many people just waiting by the tables of the many cafés in the square. The seats by the tables were full and she was lucky to find somewhere to sit, but she noticed that, although many people had cups of espresso coffee, or ice-creams, others, even the waiters, seemed to be waiting for something to happen in the cathedral.

A waiter dusted off the crumbs from the table and Samantha ordered fresh orange juice and soda water. The sun poured down, and she was glad of the wide floppy linen hat that kept the worst of the heat from her head and neck as she relaxed for the first time since she came to Italy two days ago.

The cold drink made the glass frosty, and she let her wrist touch it lightly to cool her pulse. Her table was close to the cathedral steps, and she wished that it was further back, away from the crowd that passed and re-passed the bottom of the steps, scattered at times by a moped or two that seemed to be a natural but noisy addition to the life of Amalfi. The young mother and child who sat at the same table ignored her, intent on watching the cathedral steps, and there was an air of expectancy.

A horse-drawn carriage with open top and bright trimmings on the harness stood at one side of the steps, and a group of beautifully dressed men and women lingered by its side, many with cameras, and all laughing.

Of course! It's a wedding, Samantha realised, and looked more closely at the group of people who now stood ready in a position to take really good pictures of whoever it was who would walk down that long stairway. Two men had video cameras and there were at least three more who Samantha thought were professional photographers, neatly but soberly dressed as if this was just another wedding assignment. The clothes of the wedding party were chic and very expensive, and the style was so obviously Italian couture that she was filled with something akin to envy.

Sleek cars took up most of the roadway leading to the café area and more people walked down through the town to join the party.

How good-looking they are, she thought. Dark-eyed and vivacious women, and the men had an air of arrogant self-confidence, knowing how good they looked and eyeing every pretty girl in sight as routine.

Except for one! Samantha watched him walk down the road, his hands tense at his sides and his head held high as if to keep his explosive emotions under control. He was as dark as the other men, but as he passed by, without a glance to right or left, she saw that he had deep blue eyes; not brown as most

Italian eyes were, but a blue that was almost violet, now cold and angry and almost frightening. His suit was less flamboyant than the rest, and was not of Italian cut, and he lacked the heavy gold rings that the other men wore.

He's not married or he'd wear a wedding ring, she decided, and blushed slightly. It was none of her business if he had six wives. He stood at the foot of the steps, gazing up at the empty archway, and if she had leaned forward she could have touched him. Suddenly confused, and hoping that he had not seen her staring, she sipped her drink and tried to look away, but found that of all the faces in that crowd his was the only one she wanted to watch.

A sound that was partly a cry of anticipation and partly a sigh at the sudden vision of loveliness that appeared at the top of the cathedral steps swelled up to meet the bride. Samantha caught her breath and forgot the man, who now stood quite still, his hands limp at his sides, as if suddenly bereft of feeling. The girl was exquisite. Dark abundant hair, entwined with flowers, was framed by a delicate lace veil that floated after her to mingle with the long diaphanous train. Her slender waist, so small that it looked as if it could break from the weight of the heavy silk skirt, supported the richly embroidered bodice, and she walked slowly down to the square, her bridegroom slightly behind her, as if aware that this was her day and he was just part of the scene.

Step by step, they came closer, the pure white chiffon billowing behind them, gently touching the scarlet carpet covering the centre of the stairway, and the girl's face was alight with joy.

Samantha looked away as the bridal pair climbed into the open carriage and women fussed over the yards and yards of veiling to make sure it avoided touching the wheels. Cameras clicked and flashed, and the child sitting at the table pulled her mother's jeans and dragged her away to watch the carriage disappear, but the man who sank on to the now vacant seat at Samantha's table held no camera, and just stared after the departing carriage with sombre eyes.

The crowd moved away, the sleek cars filled and followed the carriage up the hill to the huge hotel that had the space and elegance for a wedding reception, and the excitement was over. Samantha lowered her gaze and found that she had finished her drink. She glanced back at the café, and the waiter saw her and came over. She hesitated to ask for the bill and leave as she had enjoyed the drink and found it refreshing. She wanted to sit for an hour to watch the centre of Amalfi and everything that went on around her, but she couldn't sit there calmly, opposite this controlled volcano, as if he didn't exist.

'*Ancora, signorina*?' the waiter asked. She nodded. She would do as she had intended and stay. Why should she be intimidated by one very cross man who had not even noticed her presence? '*Per il signore*?' the man asked, and Samantha saw the blue eyes register her for the first time.

'We aren't together,' she said hastily in English, and the waiter looked blank.

The mobile mouth softened and a few phrases of soft Italian explained that he too would have the fruit drink. Samantha looked across the square at the statue of St Andrew and tried to admire it, but the saint looked very bored and the cherubs round his feet were far too fat to be attractive.

'Ghastly, isn't it?' The very English voice startled her, and her eyes widened. 'Never pretend to admire something just because it's old and famous,' he said. 'There are so many beautiful statues and buildings here on the Almafian coast that you'll soon have your fill of beauty without having to waste time on trash.'

'St Andrew wouldn't be very flattered,' she replied, and relaxed.

'He didn't make the statue. He'd have hated it. A gentle man whom the sailors adopted as their patron saint,' he added.

'I know,' Samantha said. 'I did a little homework before I came to Italy so that I could see the really interesting things.'

'Not joining the package coach tours? Very wise. Much more fun to take a ticket on a boat or a bus, or hire a car if you've the courage to take on the manic Italian drivers, who all seem to have a death-wish.'

She smiled. Was this the man who half an hour ago had been so filled with such anger, and—yes, a kind of sorrow, that he seemed about to do something dramatic? Talking casually as she would to any fellow-countryman met in a café abroad, she found him interesting and amusing and very attractive. She swallowed some of the icy cold fluid and instinctively put a hand to her throat as if expecting the swallowing to make it sore, but found no trace of pain now, three weeks after she'd had her tonsils removed.

'Sore?' he asked. 'Be careful in this heat, and make sure you never get chilled after dark.' For a moment he looked sombre again, then he smiled. 'You don't want to "see Naples and die", do you? OK, I know it doesn't mean that literally, and we needn't spell it out, but if you do have a sore throat here, get something for it before it takes a hold and ruins your holiday, or worse.'

'It isn't sore now. I lost my tonsils a few weeks ago and I still expect to feel it. Just habit, but I can't believe that it's really better after months of vague tonsillitis,' she said.

'Oh, where was this?'

'In London, at the Princess Beatrice Hospital.'

'None better,' he replied. 'I know it well.'

She laughed. 'I suppose everyone who knows London knows Beattie's. That seems ages ago now, and I want to forget it. This is another world, and I have a month here to live a life of utter self-indulgence.'

'Alone?' The blue eyes challenged her and she hid her own under long eyelashes.

'Independently, but not really alone, I'm staying at a villa away above the bay.'

'Where?'

She looked at him with less warmth. Was this the prelude to a pick-up?

'Near San Antonio,' she said with an air of finality. 'You're right about the driving here. It does need a lot of concentration.'

He grinned as if reading her thoughts and she

tugged at her hat to bring it further over her eyes. 'It's far too hot now,' he said firmly. 'From your slightly English sickroom pallor, I'd advise lunch and a rest this afternoon, and perhaps a visit to Ravello this evening.'

Samantha raised her eyebrows. 'Do you organise every stranger you meet?' she queried.

'Only the ones with big green eyes and no hair,' he said. 'I can see no curly locks under that awful hat, but it's the first time I met anyone who had a head shaved for tonsillectomy!'

'It's a very practical hat, and one that Sir Ralph's wife gave me, with strict instructions to wear it when I was out in the sun.' She bit her lip as she saw his curiosity at the mention of a name.

'Are they over here now?' he asked.

'Who?' she asked coldly.

'Sir Ralph Gower, of course. I assume you're staying in their villa near San Antonio,' he replied calmly, as if spelling out something to a rather dim child.

'That's right,' she said slowly. 'Do you know them?'

'Everyone who's been to San Antonio knows the Gowers,' he replied, and she sensed that he regretted mentioning them. He stood up abruptly, and signalled to the waiter to bring the check, waving aside Samantha's efforts to pay her share. 'You probably saved my sanity,' he said, 'so the least I can do is to pay for your lemonade.' His voice was hard and he looked as he had done when Samantha had first seen him, tense and hurt and angry.

'Thank you,' was all she could say, and hesitated, at a loss and somehow unable just to walk away.

'Come on. Have you ever seen an Italian wedding reception?' She shook her head. 'Organised chaos,' he said, and smiled sadly. 'They'll never notice one extra, and I have to be there, like it or not. I couldn't get to the wedding, but at least I'll drink to her health and happiness.' He half turned away and Samantha wondered if he really did add, 'If that's possible, poor darling.'

'I can't go there! I don't even know you, and I couldn't gatecrash a wedding!'

He looked at her jeans and long bright batik tunic shirt and the floppy hat. 'No, maybe not,' he agreed. 'But as we nearly do know each other because of Sir Ralph, I can't let you wander about here on your own all day, and I need someone. . .after the reception.' He laughed softly. 'I'll arrange lunch for you on the balcony bar overlooking the party, and you can watch the antics of the average Italian at play! I'll join you as soon as I can, and we can take it from there.'

'But I have no intention of wasting time watching a party of people I don't know! I don't know you either, and I'd feel out of it and very embarrassed!'

'Then let's get acquainted. 'I'm—er—Laurie Martin, and you are?'

'Samantha Croft,' she said.

He held out a hand and raised her fingertips to his lips. 'Welcome to Italy, Samantha.' He released her hand quickly as if the polite touch was enough and he wanted no further contact, and she had a sneaky feeling that he had hesitated too long before saying his name, as if he wasn't telling the truth, but her fingers tingled and she knew that she had wanted him to hold her hand and keep it close.

'I can't——' she began again.

'I'll drive you back to San Antonio later,' he offered.

'I have my own wheels,' she replied. 'I parked up there on the rise of the hill.'

'Couldn't be better. That's near the hotel,' he said, and led her from the square and over the crossing to the port.

Samantha took a deep breath that wasn't filled with diesel fumes and looked out at the fishing boats along the jetty and the smart yachts anchored out in the bay. She hung her leather holdall over one shoulder and put on dark glasses. 'This is a wonderful coast,' she remarked. 'I'd hoped to swim today, but the water doesn't look very clean inshore. Would it be better out by the jetty?' she asked with regret.

'Swim here? You must be crazy! With your surgical history you mustn't swim in anything but a very clean pool for a while, and in the Bay of Naples, never!' He urged her on by pointing out various boats, and landmarks like the old Saracen tower above the town on a rocky outcrop near the hotel. 'What's wrong with the pool at the villa?' he asked. 'That should be clean enough for anyone. Sir Ralph is a bit fussy about such things.'

'Then you really do know the villa? More than just because you've visited San Antonio and Sir Ralph is a popular figure there?'

'Yes, I've known them for years and worked with Sir Ralph for six months.'

'But he's a surgeon!'

'That's right.' Laurie Martin sounded amused. 'At Beattie's, where you were a patient.'

'I've never met you there,' she said, puzzled.

'Why should you? How long were you in there? A few days? A week at most? Even a bad peritonsillar abscess would respond in that time with antibiotics and surgery, and I don't do ear, nose and throat surgery. In fact, I've moved to Beattie's only this year from Guy's. Sir Ralph operates there too, and he suggested the job of registrar when it came vacant at Easter.'

Samantha leaned against the wall to let another car rush by as they walked up the hill. 'I'm in my last year at Beattie's,' she said. 'I've been nursing on night duty for the past three months and that's what made me vulnerable to the throat infection which I picked up from the children's ward.'

'Nasty streppy things, kids,' he remarked, and she turned back to look at him.

'They aren't. I loved every minute there,' she said, and blushed, realising that he was teasing her. 'Apart from when they coughed all over me, and one little boy really did have a very virulent streptococcal infection which he shared freely!'

'No theatre work for you until you have three clear throat swabs?' he asked. 'That's if you like operating theatres.'

'That's exactly what I want to do, and I was lined up for it before this happened. They've been very good to keep the option open, and this is the reason for all this time off—sick leave and some holiday tagged on to make sure I can go into theatre if I pass my final exams. I'm waiting for the results now. Sir Ralph had a few cases in Kids and seemed to think he'd like me back in general surgery theatre, so he offered me this break if I'd just stay at the villa to keep an eye on his two teenagers, in case they bring in friends who might break up the place.' She shrugged. 'I feel like a spy, and I'm sure they aren't likely to cause any aggro, but I've only met them once, as they're both enrolled in a language school that takes up most of their day time.'

'Cross now!' Laurie Martin took her hand and rushed her across the busy road, and before she could resist and go to her car she was inside the cool blue and white tiled hallway of the hotel, a haven after the hot and dusty road.

'I can't stay here,' she insisted.

'You must.' He turned her to face him in the cool, dim alcove by the entrance and his fingers dug into her arms. 'Please, Samantha, I need to talk in English and to be with a woman who's completely different from those up there. I need to be Laurie Martin.'

She swayed towards him as his grip tightened, and for a moment she thought he was about to kiss her. She drew away, but gently, thinking that he was moving too fast, and yet she could feel no annoyance, but rather a growing awareness of his masculinity and a feeling that they must have met in another life. If this was just a vulgar pick-up, it didn't feel like it, and she knew that she wanted to see him again.

The clean, coloured floor tiles of ancient ceramic made soft slappings under her sandalled feet, and in another minute she was rising in the elevator. She found herself deposited in a comfortable chair overlooking the sea, and when she looked down over the balcony she could watch the wedding party, as the awnings were thrown back to make the open room light and airy.

'Don't go away,' Laurie commanded. 'I've told Luigi to give you what you want as one of the wedding guests. I explained that you've come straight from the airport and so you can't appear with the others as there's been a hitch about luggage.'

'Do you tell many lies with such conviction?' she asked.

'Not many, but when I do it has to be good. I have to go. *Buon appetito*!'

The waiter filled her glass with dry white wine, and she asked for mineral water to drink as well as she had to drive after lunch. The melon and Parma ham was delicious, and it was at least five minutes later that she glanced down at the party below. It was quieter now as everyone was eating, and she saw that Laurie Martin was sitting at the top table with the bridal party. When he spoke to the others, his hands moved with expression, in the Italian manner, and he looked just like one of the other Italian guests, apart from his style of dress and his deep blue eyes.

Laurie Martin? Somehow that didn't sound right now that he was with these people, and Samantha recalled his hesitation when he revealed his name. What am I doing here? she asked herself. She shook

back her mane of bronzy gold hair, freshly brushed
out after its confinement under the hat.

As soon as she was alone at her table she had
asked for the ladies' room, and now she felt tidy and
cool after immersing her hands in cold water, and
freshening her make-up.

I'm Samantha Croft, level-headed staff nurse from
the Princess Beatrice Hospital in London, where I
do very responsible work and enjoy a good and
varied social life. I have lots of dates that I can
handle, and the choice of at least two very eligible
men who want me more than I want them, which
until now has made life easy, she told herself.

Until now? It was a scaring thought that a meeting
with a stranger whom she didn't really trust could
make any difference to her life.

Samantha gazed down at the now almost silent
scene. Speeches were being said, or orated, if the
gesticulations were any hint of what was being said.
She smiled. They were having a ball! Another burst
of applause greeted Laurie Martin, who stood with
a champagne glass in his hand, turning it by the stem
between hard fingers as if he were about to break it.
Samantha listened to the deep, pleasant voice and
the fluent Italian that poured without effort or pause
from his sensitive mouth.

Faces turned to him were smiling, but Samantha
had the impression that several guests at the top
table looked relieved, as if they had expected him to
say something more than was required at such a
gathering. At last he held up his glass and looked
directly at the bride. His voice grew softer and his
expression was sad and full of love. He wished her

health and happiness, then sat down, draining his glass and filling it again from the champagne bottle before him.

Samantha sat back and ate her ice-cream, knowing she must stay now and make sure Laurie Martin did not drive. At least three glasses of champagne and the wine drunk with the meal added up to a lethal cocktail for anyone driving a car. In vain she told herself that he was a stranger and not her responsibility, but she was still sitting on the balcony when Luigi, the head waiter, told her that Signor Martinello was waiting downstairs. She smiled, wondering what Luigi could make of her name. Signorina Croft really didn't lend itself to being translated into Italian.

Down below, the bride was once more being subjected to a photographic session and was wilting visibly. It must be difficult to smile to order, twenty times in a row, and to look happy all the time. Samantha felt a great deal of sympathy for the girl, who had listened to Laurie Martin with tears in her eyes as if deeply affected, and now looked pale and fragile as if a breath of wind might blow her away.

'Sorry it took so long.' Laurie Martin stared. 'You *do* have hair. *Bella*!' he said, with an exaggerated bow.

'May I go now?' she asked.

'You may, but I have to ask a favour. Drive me home?'

Samantha breathed a sigh of relief. So often the most macho of men would never accept that they were not fit to drive. 'Sure,' she said, in a businesslike tone. 'Let's go. You'll have to navigate. Which road do we take? Are you staying near Amalfi?'

'I'm booked in at a hotel where a lot of the wedding guests are staying, but frankly I can't take any more of that today. I know Sir Ralph would put me up even before I'm due to arrive at the villa to see him, so let's go home.'

'What about your clothes? A toothbrush and a hairbrush might be useful; and pyjamas?'

'Right, turn off here and I'll collect all my luggage and pay the bill.' He grinned. 'Yes, Nurse! I do clean my teeth and wash behind my ears, but no pyjamas. I sleep raw.'

Samantha pursed her lips and stopped the car outside another luxury hotel, and ten minutes later he emerged, carrying a large leather bag as if he would be staying at the villa for ages. She recalled that Sir Ralph had mentioned that he would fly over for a few days on business, and she hoped he would be glad to see an uninvited guest.

Laurie Martin leaned back and closed his eyes, while Samantha had no time to think about anything but negotiating the sharp bends and avoiding the many small cars which were driven with more verve than accuracy, and had the dents to prove it. The hills rose before them, and the traffic eased as the car followed side-roads, and soon the Villa Stresa was in sight, nestling among trees and ablaze with scarlet geraniums and purple bougainvillaeas.

'Well done,' her passenger said sleepily. 'I'll find an empty room in the annexe over there. It's all right, don't look so anxious. That's where Sir Ralph

puts odd surgeons and doctors who meet him here,
so they aren't under the feet of his family all day.'

'And you're an odd surgeon?' she asked with a
smile as she decided that he really did know the villa
and would be welcome there.

'Very odd just now. I think I could use some black
coffee. I'll be over on the terrace as soon as you've
made it,' he added calmly.

'I'll ask Maria. I haven't been allowed in the
kitchen yet, and I'd hate to upset her.'

'Ask her if she has any of those little doughnuts
she makes. See you.'

Samantha walked away, and was conscious that
he stared after her and lingered by the car until she
had gone.

'Sarah? Is everything all right? I thought you were
in language school today.' Samantha regarded Sir
Ralph's seventeen-year-old daughter with a frown.

'It's too hot, and I didn't feel like it,' the girl
replied, her chin jutting out aggressively. 'I suppose
you want to check up on Mark too?'

'Why should I? If you want to waste valuable time
and fail your exams next year, it's no skin off my
nose,' Samantha said airily. 'I'm here to get fit
enough to do the work for which I've been trained,
and I've no time to wet-nurse two spoiled kids.' She
walked quickly away to the kitchen and asked Maria
for coffee.

Maria frowned. 'For the *signorina*? She has had
coffee. Two coffee.'

'No. For me and for Dr Martin, who says he'll
stay here in the annexe to wait for Sir Ralph,'

Samantha said, slowly so that Maria could understand her English.

'*Si! Per il signore* I put the cakes he likes.' Maria beamed and hurried over to the cupboard and piled tiny cakes covered with icing on to a large plate. 'Take, and I will bring coffee to the terrace,' she said, and Samantha felt dismissed.

Laurie Martin was sitting under a tree with his feet on another chair and his eyes half shut. He had changed from the formal suit and now wore a pair of rust-coloured baggy trousers and an acid lemon Sea Island cotton shirt open at the neck, revealing a disc of gold on a slender gold chain that nestled among the dark hairs of his chest.

'Good, I need some blotting paper,' he said, and took three of the small cakes.

'After a four-course meal?' Samantha asked, laughing. 'I refused the pasta as being too filling, and even three courses were more than enough for me in the middle of the day.'

He paused with a half-eaten cake in his hand. 'I'm hungry. You might not have noticed, but I hardly touched the food.'

'I noticed that the bride didn't seem hungry, and that's usual, I believe, but as I wasn't getting married and had no butterflies in my stomach I enjoyed my lunch very much.'

'Butterflies? Is that what I had?'

'Coffee!' Maria put the tray on the table and stood back to look at him. Samantha listened, and gathered from the exchange of rapid Italian that Maria would make his favourite food for him and yes, he was enjoying her most beautiful cakes.

Maria went away, back to the appetising smells issuing from the kitchen, and Laurie groaned. 'I shall put on kilos. She cooks like a dream and force-feeds me.'

'At least you have no speech to give now, so the butterflies can fly away,' Samantha said, smiling. 'You can eat and grow fat. That's if you're staying for long?'

'Sir Ralph has shares in a clinic here and we may do a few operations over the next week or so. I'm covered for my work at Beattie's and decided to combine business with—what? I can't call it pleasure. Yes, I suppose I'm here for the wedding: the all-important wedding that should never have happened.'

'What do you mean?' Samantha put down the coffee-pot and stared. 'The bride looked lovely, and she seemed blissfully happy when she came down the cathedral steps.'

'I did notice!' The voice was hard again and the blue eyes cold. 'For how long?'

'For life, I think,' replied Samantha. 'The groom looked handsome and caring. He has a good mouth and eyes, and he never took his gaze from her during the speeches, as if he wanted to gather her up and take her away before it was over.'

'For life? How long is life?'

'What's wrong?' she asked. 'Don't you like the bridegroom? Is he a villain or a fortune-hunter? Married before?'

'None of those things. I like Paolo. He's wealthy and can afford the very best for Caterina, and you're right—she is in love with him and will go with him wherever he takes her, however unsuitable.'

'I don't understand. You made a good speech and toasted her health and future happiness, and yet you're all uptight about it.'

'I pray that she'll be happy and enjoy life. After all, the quality of life is more important than the length, so if her happiness lasts for, say, six months, then what matters after that?'

'Somehow I get the impression that you have no time for marriage,' Samantha said, seething with annoyance. 'Some marriages last and grow even better with the years. How could you stand up and speak as you did, with every sign of sincerity, in front of a hundred people, when you were secretly being so cynical? Don't you believe in true love?'

'Of course I believe in love.' He gave a cold half-smile. 'I believe in all kinds of love: the love of children and parents, the love between friends, love that can be bought and sold but legalised in marriage and love that's real for a while but doomed to failure.'

'She is in love,' Samantha insisted. 'He looks the ideal husband, and they'll be happy. You said he's wealthy and caring and that you like him, so I can't see any problem.'

'Fortunately it's not your problem,' he replied coldly. 'There are matters that don't concern you and about which you know nothing, so stop looking so angry.' He took a deep breath as if trying to be pleasant and to take the sting from his words. He smiled. 'You remind me of the dragon in Casualty at Beattie's. She looks at all the doctors like that.

You're far too pretty to become like her. Really, this isn't an issue for you, Samantha. I know about Caterina. I love her and want her to be happy.'

'You say that, but in reality you want that marriage to fail.'

'I want very sincerely for her to have health and happiness,' he said earnestly. 'But that marriage shouldn't have happened. She has married the wrong man.' He gulped the rest of his coffee and strode away over the terrace to the cottage annexe, and Samantha was left alone.

The wrong man? she thought. If Paolo was the wrong man then who was the right one? Her coffee suddenly tasted bitter and half cold, and she wished she had never sat at that café table by the cathedral. Laurie Martin was in love with the bride, and was so bitter about it that it coloured his whole idea of her marriage.

She sighed. Yesterday I was looking forward to staying here and getting really fit, without a care in the world, and now I shall have to spend my time avoiding him.

CHAPTER TWO

'HELLO, I'm Jenny.' The girl sounded listless.

Samantha brought her mind back to the present and smiled. 'Hello. I didn't hear you, and I was far away.'

'I know the feeling.' The girl sat on the parapet wall overlooking the garden and the pool, and her pale face indicated that she was a new arrival from somewhere less sunny than Italy. 'I'm Sarah's friend from college,' she explained. 'I came this afternoon, and I wish I was back at home.'

'Why is that? The sun shines, the water in the pool there looks tempting and I can smell a wonderful meal being produced by someone other than me, and we don't have to do a thing.' Who am I trying to convince? Samantha considered. It's all true, but I feel as she does—that I wish I'd never come here.

'You'll soon settle in,' she said. 'You know Sarah and Mark, and we seem to have other visitors who you may find interesting. The views are marvellous—we can see Vesuvius from the upstairs windows. I came yesterday and I still can't believe I'm here,' she added, trying to sound enthusiastic.

'I think the plane upset me, and the drive from the airport was very bumpy,' Jenny explained.

'Did you come by coach? They do sway about on these roads,' Samantha said.

'No, Sarah asked someone to meet the plane and he brought me here.'

'Oh? You mean Dr Martin?' Samantha felt her facial muscles tighten. She had seen nothing of Laurie Martin since he strode away in a bad mood yesterday, and now she wondered if he had left the villa. The sound of wheels on the drive last evening had told her that she wouldn't see him at dinner, and there was no sign of his car today. An evening meal with two rather silent and bored teenagers hadn't been fun, and she had gone to her room as soon as it was polite to do so.

'No. Who's he? A man who Mark met in England turned up in Ravello and phoned Sarah, so she asked him to fetch me and come here today. He's around somewhere,' Jenny said with a complete lack of interest.

'Another student?' Samantha tried not to be disappointed. So there was no sign of Laurie Martin. The man she had met and who had made an uncomfortably deep impression on her might even now be flying away, back to England to forget the unhappy memories of the girl he loved being married to another man. She sighed inwardly. It was just as well that he had left her life before he had really entered it.

'Older than usual. I think he's got one degree and is trying for a Master's in psychology.' Jenny shrugged. 'Great if you like big blond macho guys from the US of A.'

'But you don't?' Samantha laughed. 'You sound very bored with life. Was he that ugly? Or married with six children?'

'He's OK, but at this moment if you served up Sylvester Stallone on ice, I'd turn away!' Jenny levered herself off the wall as if very weary.

'You really are ill!' Samantha took the limp wrist and felt the rapid and thready pulse-rate. The girl felt hot and her skin was dry, and on inspection her eyes looked dull and sunken. 'When did this come on? Not just on the plane,' Samantha persisted.

'No, it came on when I was leaving home, but I'd been busy and I'm near the end of my period, and that gets me down a bit. I'll take a shower and change and I'll be better. I seem to have stomach cramps now, and that's a bit unusual for me.' Listlessly Jenny turned away, then paused. 'Do you have a couple of tampons I could use? I seem to be fresh out of them.'

'Sure. I'll get some.' Samantha was glad of an excuse to stay with the girl, who was beginning to worry her now. 'Any real pain?' she asked.

'A tight feeling here,' Jenny said, pointing to her lower abdomen, 'and yes—ouch! It hurts all over when I prod it.' She walked slowly as if every step was a supreme effort.

'I'll stay in your room while you shower. That is if you feel up to having a shower.' Samantha saw the pallor increase and the eyes looked hot with fever. 'Stay in your room until I bring the tampons.'

'Could you hand one in to me in the loo? After that, I'll have a shower. I feel grubby and a bit smelly. I ought to have put in a fresh one yesterday, but as I said, I ran out and thought I could buy some here.'

'Yesterday?' echoed Samantha.

Jenny looked embarrassed. 'Well, the day before. I'm not losing much and I often don't change all that often when it's the end of a period. They cost a lot, and I'm only a student!' she added defensively. She walked along the corridor to the bathroom, and Samantha hurried to get what was needed.

A crash and a groan made her run, and she pushed on the unlocked door of the toilet. Jenny lay in a heap and an offensive smell pervaded the atmosphere. Samantha resisted the urge to pull the handle to flush away the soiled tampon in the toilet bowl, and covered the seat before she half dragged Jenny into the corridor. The girl was semi-conscious and heavy, but somehow Samantha managed to get her on to her bed, pulled off her jeans and placed a towel between her legs, then found a large plastic bag to cover her own hand, took a deep breath and fished out the soggy tampon, which she sealed in the bag.

The house was silent and apart from Mark and Sarah, who could be anywhere, she had no idea who to ask for help. 'Maria?' she called, and shouted again from the head of the stairs. 'Someone! Anyone! Help!' Still no sound. She glanced back into the room where Jenny was breathing with soft, shallow, rapid breaths. Samantha ran down to the kitchen and thrust open the door. She gulped, her small store of Italian lost as Maria looked up from a bowl of dough that would finally emerge as delicious pizza. '*Signorina* is sick. . .*malata.*' Oh, why do I speak French and not Italian? she wondered. '*Dove il signore*? Dottore Martin?' she managed.

Maria pointed in the general direction of the

annexe and went on with her kneading. Samantha
fled and hammered on the door of the cottage. From
an inner room she heard a male voice singing an aria
from a Puccini opera. It might be from the radio,
but it did mean there was someone at home. She
knocked again and found a rather rusty bell-pull at
the side of the door, which she tugged until a loud
bell rang loud enough to alert Pavarotti or whoever
was soaring up to the high notes, and the force of
her pulling made the bell knob come away in her
hand.

The door was flung open, and Samantha looked
at the broken wire in her hand and then at the man
who faced her.

Laurie Martin clutched a bath towel round his
waist with one hand and the other was raised in an
arc as he finished his aria with a flourish, then
realised who was there at the door. 'You?' he said,
and only just saved his towel as he instinctively put
out his right hand to greet her. 'Come in. This is a
pleasant surprise. I meant to get presentable and ask
you to come for a drive.' Beads of moisture rain-
bowed his dark hair and his chest was glistening and
brown as he rubbed it nearly dry with the other
small towel he had held and waved at the climax of
the aria.

'Please come,' she said urgently, and looked away,
shocked at her reaction to his near-naked body.

'Just as I am?' He grinned, and she wished she
could touch the strong line of his jaw and the tender
promise of his mouth. 'Here, sit down on the bench.
You're badly out of breath,' he said severely. 'I
thought you were an invalid.'

'It's Jenny,' she said.

'Jenny who?'

'A friend of Sarah's who arrived just now. She's very ill and I don't know who to ask for help! I managed to get her to bed, but she's getting worse all the time and needs treatment.'

'*Andiamo,*' he said, and ran back into the cottage, emerging a minute later in a pair of brief swimming-trunks that made him look very Italian. 'Tell me what happened,' he said as they hurried back to the main house.

Samantha stifled an absurd desire to giggle, partly with relief and partly because a man in brief trunks with a stethoscope round his neck looked a trifle odd. 'She has a fever and a very rapid pulse and her respirations are poor,' she panted, trying to keep up with him.

'Pain?' he asked.

'Lower abdomen, and a lot of guarding when I touched her. She says it's tender all over. She's almost unconscious.'

'Right. We need an ambulance, but I'll see her first. If she's very bad, a journey over these roads might not be advisable, and I might have to do it here.'

'Do what?'

'Classic case, from what you tell me. Full marks for observation,' he said, in a way that made her feel like a first-year nursing auxiliary who had been patted on the head for noticing that someone had a cold!

'You think it might be an appendix?' she asked as

they reached the room and saw Jenny moaning on the bed.

'What else? Maybe even have ruptured. We may have to move fast,' Laurie added grimly as he put away the stethoscope and held Jenny's wrist in his strong fingers.

Samantha tensed her whole body as if afraid of being attacked. 'It's not appendix,' she said clearly.

'She told you she'd had it out?' He regarded her with disbelief. 'It's true that I can't ask her if it's more painful over the right iliac fossa, which would clinch the diagnosis, but all the rest is there.'

'I think it's toxic shock syndrome,' Samantha said, and waited for the sky to fall on her. At Beattie's, she knew that the more masculine a doctor seemed, the more he resented being told his diagnosis was wrong, and if it was a nurse who hadn't even gained her certificate who said such a thing, then she might have to run for her life!

He swung the stethoscope as if about to lasso a calf and smiled coldly. 'If I accept your diagnosis, Nurse, then she will not have an operation, and she'll have fast medication which may or may not cure her, but if you're wrong and I don't operate, she'll die. I can't ask the patient anything, and I have only what I see and can palpate, and time's running out. I have to get an anaesthetist out here fast, and you'll have to help me.'

'Wait! I have something to show you,' she said, and brought in the plastic bag and a thick wadge of newspaper on to which she discharged the contents. 'She had this *in situ* for at least two if not three days, and she did manage to tell me the brand name of the tampon. It's a brand that was held in some disrepute last year and was taken from the shelves because it gives out gases when soiled and is dangerous if it's not changed often. They're officially banned as there were several deaths in the United States, but you know what happens—people buy them up from unscrupulous suppliers and they appear on the market. She probably bought them cheap from a market stall or wherever, and didn't know that they give off toxic chemicals when they're left in for too long a time.'

'I heard about those cases in the States,' Laurie said. He looked at the specimen more closely. 'Typical signs,' he acceded. 'Typical history, with that very sudden onset of symptoms, but this tampon is certainly what really convinces me you're right.' He prodded the malodorous mess with a pencil that he took from the table. 'Now what do we do?' he asked with an air of great innocence.

Samantha looked up sharply and blushed. 'I don't know,' she admitted. 'Penicillin?' she asked hopefully.

'Thank God you don't know everything,' he said, and laughed. 'Fortunately for the human race, I carry a little of everything when I'm away from a good modern hospital, and what I haven't got with me I shall find in Sir Ralph's office. Penicillin isn't the answer for this, as this infection is usually penicillin-resistant. He has a minor dispensary in there to which he gave me a key.' He looked at the ashen face again. 'A cool sponge, with care not to shock, I think.'

'Yes, Doctor,' she answered meekly, but the

corners of her mouth twitched with rising elation.
She had been right, and he wasn't furious with her.

'Fetch my bag from the cottage,' he ordered. 'I
have several sterile syringes in it and a few spirit
swabs in a jar. We must get a big initial injection of
Methicillin sodium into her and hope for the best
before we have the path report.'

Samantha hurried back, and he opened the
syringe and the phial of the drug. 'Hold her arm
still,' he said as Jenny began to turn on the bed and
to draw up her knees into the foetal position. He
injected, then regarded his patient with a deep
frown. 'I hope to God it works,' he muttered. 'I'm a
surgeon and I can't say I've ever seen this condition
before now, except in theory.' He looked up. 'Have
you met it before this one?'

'Yes. We had a girl from a hippie commune
brought into Casualty with these symptoms, and the
casualty officer thought she had acute venereal dis-
ease until he did an examination per vagina and
found one like that, only worse, inside.' Samantha
bit her lip and glanced at Jenny, but said no more as
it was possible that Jenny could hear what was being
said, and she had no intention of adding to her
troubles by saying that the girl had died from toxic
absorption.

'Someone must drive to Naples and leave the
specimen in for examination, but it's almost certainly
a staphylococcal infection, and so I've given her an
umbrella type of anti-staph that won't do her any
harm and may save her life.'

'I have a car,' she said.

'No, not you. I need you here to keep a check on

her condition and to keep her temperature down, and if the sponging rouses her make her take these tablets. I can't give sodium fusidate by intramuscular injection. It has to be by drip or by mouth, so do your best, as we haven't a drip set here.' Laurie indicated a couple of tablets. 'She may have a rigor, and a lay person would be scared and useless.' He thought for a moment. 'Someone who speaks Italian might help, and certainly someone who can drive on these roads and not get lost, so that rules out Mark and Sarah.'

'What about the man who collected Jenny from the airport? She said he's older than the other students, and he did manage the roads with no trouble.'

'Find him, while I pack this specimen and write clear instructions to the pathologist.' He sat by the bed and took out a pen, and when Samantha came back with a puzzled Nathan Stenner, who stared at the comatose figure on the bed as if he just couldn't believe his eyes, Laurie Martin had the note ready.

'How's your Italian?' he asked.

'Not bad,' Nathan admitted.

'You get the picture? She's very sick and I need that report. Can you get it to the lab and then pick up this list of drugs from the pharmacy? They know me and will give you every assistance, but hurry, as she's going to need them if the infection isn't what I think it is. I've added the phone number of this place, and the lab can ring through when they have a preliminary result and the pathologist's own opinion if he's met this before today, but I'm afraid some tests will take a day or so, and we haven't much time to waste.'

'Sure, I'll go,' Nathan said, and took the package to his car, without wasting time on questions.

Samantha fetched a plastic bowl from the kitchen and filled it with cool water. A large sponge that Laurie supplied from his bathroom, and plenty of soft towels, made it possible to give Jenny a tepid sponge, taking only one limb at a time and allowing the moisture to dry on each limb in turn, patting it with a towel and covering it before starting on another. Between each sponging she took Jenny's temperature in her axilla so that she could notice any sudden and shocking fall in the body temperature, and she avoided sponging her chest and abdomen.

Samantha blessed her tutor at Beattie's, who had insisted that they learn such techniques in case they were ever in a situation such as a Third World country where modern drugs were not available and fever was present. At the time the students had grumbled that they would never have to use methods straight from the Ark, but she valued the lecture now. She recalled that it was necessary to stop sponging when the temperature had fallen not quite far enough, as afterwards it would fall another degree or so with no further treatment, and so must not be brought down too quickly, to avoid shock.

Jenny half opened her eyes. 'That's good,' she murmured. Samantha held a cup of mineral water to the girl's lips and she drank greedily. She even managed to swallow the tablets, and Samantha made a note of the time when she took them. Her temperature was still high, but not as worrying now, and the chance of a rigor receded. It seemed impossible that a healthy girl should collapse so quickly.

Laurie came back, dressed more soberly in light trousers and a deep blue T-shirt. He lounged in the doorway while Samantha cleared away the bowl but left the towels hanging out to dry on the balcony ready for the next treatment. As she wrote the details in the roughly made chart she had constructed, she was conscious of his presence and tried to move smoothly when she walked out with the bowl to empty it, but her limbs seemed uncoordinated under his gaze, and she realised that he was looking with great interest at her legs.

'I needn't have rung for an ambulance,' he said with a lazy grin. 'My, oh, my, Beattie's really do a great job.'

'They do,' she agreed coolly. 'What do you mean? Why have you sent for an ambulance? Can't Jenny stay here?'

'She could, but then I'd have two casualties on my hands,' he replied.

'I'm fine,' Samantha retorted, then knew she was really tired.

'You see?' His hand held her chin so that he could inspect the dark rings under her eyes. 'You aren't fit for such work just now. She needs care night and day for a while, and you can't do that. You're here to eat and put on as much weight as I shall do with Maria's cooking, to sit in the sun as I intend doing and to empty your mind of everything but Italy and the villa.'

'As you'll do?' she asked huskily, longing for him to forget the woman who had married another man.

'Even that,' he said, and kissed her on the mouth with such gentleness that she trembled. 'Thank you for being here, Samantha.'

'What's going on?' They heard Mark's voice in the hall. 'There's an ambulance coming up the track. Where's Nathan?'

'Send the men up here with a stretcher,' Laurie called, and Mark followed them into the room and listened intently while the ambulance men were briefed about the patient. He asked where she was being taken. 'Don't worry, she isn't having to pay,' Laurie assured him. 'As she's a guest of the family, Sir Ralph would want her to be nursed in the clinic and not in the hospital. Don't you agree, Mark? You, as his son, must give me your opinion as I'm not a member of the family, nor do I have a share in the villa, only the clinic.'

'Yes, of course she must go to the clinic. Dad would say so and so do I.' Mark braced his shoulders and looked more responsible than Samantha had noticed at breakfast, when he had slumped and eaten carelessly, looking like any other immature boy.

'Fine. Before your father arrives, you're really responsible for the welfare of your guests, not me.'

Laurie looked serious, and Mark flushed as if pleased to be thought of as an adult. 'I'll go with her if you like,' he offered. 'My Italian isn't bad now and I can find out if they want anything for her. I can hitch back or take a taxi. Is she going to be all right?' He blushed. 'She's OK when you get to know her. She's Sarah's friend,' he added hastily, as if to make sure it was known that he hadn't invited her to Italy.

'That's a load off my mind. Ring me when she's safely installed, and give this note to the sister in charge. If she wants you to stay, then perhaps you'd do that? A friendly face is important when a person feels as ill as Jenny does.'

'Is it an appendix?' asked Mark.

'No, it's a bad infection of the pelvis,' Laurie said tactfully.

Mark climbed into the ambulance, and Samantha turned away, half wishing that Jenny could remain at the villa, but admitting to herself that she wasn't fit to do heavy nursing. Her heart beat faster. Laurie Martin had noticed that she was not yet completely well, although she had been convinced she looked fine. She shrugged. It meant nothing. Doctors and nurses were trained to be observant, and he probably hadn't eyed her legs for any reason other than to notice if they were strong enough to support her!

She stripped off the bedclothes in Jenny's room and threw away the pencil that had touched the noxious specimen, then felt as if she needed a shower. Maria tapped at her bedroom door, her expression concerned. '*Il dottore* tells me all,' she said. 'Coffee on the terrace, and my nice cakes. *Il dottore* says we must feed you,' she added with satisfaction.

'I feel as if I've only just had lunch,' Samantha said, but Maria had gone.

She showered and changed into a light skirt of pastel pinks and blues and turquoise and a sleeveless silk top that toned with the turquoise and which made her eyes look more green than usual. Her leather sandals looked scuffed and heavy, so she put on light blue canvas pumps and wore no tights. It was wonderful to feel the warm air on her skin, and as she sank on to a comfortable lounger on the terrace she closed her eyes and could still sense the brightness through closed eyelids.

'Drink your coffee, or Maria will have my guts for garters.' Samantha sat up, wondering if she had dozed and not heard Maria bring the tray, but Laurie was setting it down on the white wrought-iron table. There were several cups and a large coffee-pot. A jug of cream and a bowl of coffee sugar crystals flanked a large dish of small cakes and biscuits.

'Does she always feed the five thousand?' she asked with amusement.

'I told her you'd probably saved Jenny's life, but you weren't well and needed care.' He grinned maliciously. 'I see no reason why I should be the only one to be force-fed!'

'Have you heard? Did they get to the clinic?'

'She's tucked up and they've started a drip to keep up her fluids and to introduce drugs without disturbing her. The pathologist has met such cases, and he's sure even without exhaustive tests that this is toxic shock syndrome, but of course they've put up cultures, and we shall know more tomorrow if they're growing staphs. Sister Costa is very efficient and tells me there's a decided improvement in her general condition, comparing it with your notes, for which she says a big thank you, and the pain is less, which is good news, as we can't depress her breathing too much with pain-killing drugs.'

'Poor Jenny,' Samantha murmured. 'This could really put her back a lot at college, and certainly ruin her holiday here.'

'Not to worry about that. She came away even before college came down and has a break until the autumn, unlike us poor medics and nurses who have so little free time.' Laurie took another cake and leaned back, luxuriating like a sleepy lion. No, Samantha thought, a black panther, with latent strength in those supple limbs, and a deceptive air of softness, until angered. 'You've had a messy start to your holiday,' he went on. 'I wish I could take you out to dinner, but it's more than my life is worth to leave Maria's cooking tonight, and you need an early night, but tomorrow I shall tell Maria quite firmly that you and I have to visit Jenny, which we shall do, but I shall also say we shall be out for dinner.'

'That sounds great,' Samantha said. 'Does that mean you'll be staying here for a while?' She almost held her breath, and hated being so dependent on his reply.

'For a while,' he said carelessly. 'I have to wait for Sir Ralph as we have two cases he wants me to do with him and I have a few visits to make to friends, so I shall come and go, and when I can I shall swim in the pool. Coming?' he asked.

'Now?' Samantha ran a hand over the soft warm skin of her other arm. 'I'm warm and lazy,' she said.

'You haven't eaten a cake, so you won't sink, and you need the exercise.'

'I thought I was to enjoy a lengthy and lazy convalescence,' she objected.

'Food *and* exercise,' he insisted. 'Get changed and meet me at the deep end. A quick swim will give you an appetite for dinner, and I know we could never risk swimming after a meal that Maria prepared.'

Sarah was swimming slowly, doing a leisurely breaststroke, when Samantha put one toe in the water and found to her relief that the water was warm and soft and not smelling of chlorine. Her sleek silver and emerald green bikini, a present from a fashion-conscious friend, who had told her that she never made the most of her figure, now seemed right under the hot Italian sun, and Sarah stared at her with ill-concealed envy. Laurie was making the water swirl and froth as he started on his third length, doing a stylish crawl, and Samantha slid into the water, suddenly self-conscious and wishing she'd worn a one-piece with less cleavage.

She turned on her back and floated, lazily paddling from one side of the pool to the other. At least she was sure Laurie would not make a play for her just because she was looking seductive. There was time to reflect now that the panic over Jenny was over. Laurie Martin must be made of steel, she decided. At no time since just after the wedding, when he came to the villa and recovered from the champagne he had drunk at the wedding reception, had he shown signs of the misery and depression that should rightly accompany the knowledge that his beloved had married another man. In fact, he seemed cheerful, as if he was capable of dismissing such matters from his mind, in a fatalistic way.

Sarah climbed out of the pool. 'I've done my four lengths,' she called. 'I'm hoping to put two inches on my bust, so I shall do breaststroke twice a day while I'm here. They say it's good. What do you think? Not that you need any help,' she added resentfully. 'I asked Dad about silicone implants and he went mad, but I *need* a really big bosom.'

Samantha tried not to laugh. 'You look fine, Sarah. Too much up top makes a woman look top-heavy, and it's an embarrassment when you play tennis.'

'Stop when you get to Samantha's measurements and you'll be lovely.' Laurie swam close and grinned. 'No implants, girl. Very odd-looking when you lie down, and any lover would recognise that you'd had it done, if he knew his way round female anatomy,' he added, with a wicked glance at Samantha that made her cheeks burn.

'I suppose you're an expert,' Sarah almost spat at him.

'I *am* a doctor,' he said. 'That gives me a head start.'

Sarah gave a reluctant smile. 'I'm going to change and ring the clinic. Mark's been there for ages, and I'm bored. Even Nathan has vanished.' She sat on the edge of the pool and flung back her soaking hair. 'I saw that you'd stripped Jenny's bed, and the bathroom reeks of disinfectant. What's wrong with her? Is it AIDS?'

'Why on earth would you think that was possible?' Laurie looked grim.

'No reason. She doesn't sleep around, but if she has it you'd better warn Mark. He fancies her, even if he hasn't admitted it yet, and I don't want my brother to get it.'

'Jenny has a bad pelvic infection due to poor hygiene and carelessness, but nothing as bad as AIDS, and it has no connection with any immuno-suppressive condition or any sexually transmitted disorder, so be careful and never hint at AIDS about anyone who's ill,' said Laurie sternly. 'It can cause untold damage if rumours start.' The deep blue eyes were darker than the blue of the water reflected from the blue-tiled floor of the pool, and he looked angry.

Sarah picked up her towel and turned away. 'Sorry, *signore*,' she said. 'But it's a relief, and we do worry about it in college at home, and here at the language school.' She sighed like a petulant school-girl. 'I've missed out on the permissive time. It must have been fun to do anything you wanted. Now nobody does more than heavy petting, and even then they're fussy who they kiss.'

Samantha watched her walk away, her hips sway-ing to impress them. 'If someone made a pass at her, she'd probably run away,' she said. 'Half the girls who talk so lightly about sex are frightened of it, and she's no exception. If Mark gets a girlfriend she'll feel out of it, until nature catches up with her.'

'As nature caught up with you?' It sounded an idle question, but Laurie's hand gripped the side of the pool tightly, and his neck muscles tautened as if her reply was important.

'I meet girls like that in the wards,' she explained.

'They're full of what they do and don't do, but you'd be surprised how many of them are virgins, with no experience at all.'

'Is that so?'

She laughed. 'The men are even worse—all talk and no do. In many cases, it's the ones who chat up the nurses as if they have a different girlfriend every week who are the ones who hide under the bed-clothes when they have to be examined by a woman or have treatment to any region south of the waist or umbilicus!'

He eyed her from under hooded lids, and she felt that her bikini had slipped away and in his mind she was revealed naked and vulnerable to his appraisal. 'It's strange,' he said slowly. 'In a hospital situation, people are different. We're geared to treat their illnesses or mend their broken bones, and sexuality seldom interferes with our actions and thoughts. I'd be more concerned for a woman's well-being and recovery than for her lovely sensual body.' He smiled, and Samantha felt a laser beam of tension, bright and probing, build up between them. 'Away from hospital, in the sun and near water, which in itself is aphrodisiac, I see only the beauty, and my mind becomes very unprofessional.'

He stood on the side of the pool and dived quickly into the clear water, thrusting aside the water in a racing crawl.

Samantha grabbed her towel and almost ran back to the house, breathing unevenly. She was confused. He was heartbroken, and yet there was no doubt as to how he had felt for those few minutes on the edge of the pool. As she dried her hair and changed back into less revealing clothes, she tried to be fair. He was upset by Caterina's marriage, but he was still a man, very virile and handsome, and his body responded to an attractive female as any male would do.

'But I'm not just any female!' she said aloud to herself with sadness. 'I'm me, and I want him to look at the real me, not with lust but with love.'

CHAPTER THREE

'I SAID I'd go back to the clinic. They want some of Jenny's clothes, and I offered to take them,' Mark said as if making a great sacrifice.

'That's good. She needs to be kept from feeling alone in a strange land,' said Samantha.

'Oh, *Mark*!' Sarah slammed down the magazine she had been looking at with no real enthusiasm. 'The panic's over and she'll be going home soon, and yet you've been there three times since she was admitted. Jenny's fine, and I want some fun after working hard all day.'

'You, working hard? You spend most of your time in the pool and the rest eating.' He ducked as the magazine sailed past his head. 'And you haven't been to half the lectures at the language school.'

'I talk to Maria in Italian and Nathan says I'm getting quite good, and last night, when you stayed there for absolute ages, I studied, so there.' Sarah looked resentful. 'Laurie and Samantha went off to the village for dinner, and I was left with Nathan and a bad-tempered Maria who thought we all ought to be eating here.'

'We did tell her in good time,' Samantha pointed out.

'That doesn't stop a woman like that from thinking she owns us,' Sarah said, in an annoyed voice. 'I thought I'd be free to do as I like here, but she spies on me and I'm sure she has a list of my sins to give to Mother when she sees her.'

'What's the food like at the *trattoria*?' Mark asked. 'I'll be back here for food later, but Maria's having the night off and you can run naked through the village without her having a fit if that's what turns you on! We have to get our own dinner or eat out. I think she's still in a huff about last night, and her sick aunt is just an excuse to make us pay.' He grinned. 'Shall I buy some steaks and chops and we can use the barbecue that Maria hates so much? If she's away I'd like to try it out again the way we did last year, but it's a bit off-putting when she sighs, "*Mamma mia!*" every time someone burns a chop.'

'Good idea.' Samantha spoke quickly and avoided looking at Laurie. It would be one way of making sure that they were not left alone together. 'If you get the meat in the village near the clinic, I'll go down to the shop here for any salad things we can't pick in the garden.'

'What was the trat like?' Mark asked again.

'Not bad, but crowded,' Laurie said. He glanced at Samantha. 'There was no room to move and no chance of private conversation, and the next time I invite anyone to have dinner with me I'll make sure there's at least a few centimetres' gap between tables.'

'And fewer people coming over to talk in fast Italian and drinking all our wine,' Samantha said sweetly. 'Guido really did enjoy that rather superior Barolo you ordered, and the extra bottle.'

He gave a rueful grin. 'Did you manage to have more than half a glass? He's a slob, but under that awful haircut is a very good brain when it comes to planning entertainment.'

'I didn't quite get what he was saying. I caught the bit about a procession, but not a lot more. I was afraid he was asking me to take part in something, but I hope he didn't think I was willing.'

'I apologise for last night,' said Laurie. 'Guido's organising the carnival here for June the twenty-seventh. It happens every four years, and when I was here the last time I helped a little, so he parked himself at our table last night and took over.'

'Drank far too much wine and you had to take him home in your car, dropping me off at the villa on the way,' she said in a flat voice. I'm being unfair again, she decided. What did I expect? An evening of subtle but highly charged exchanges and then perhaps an erotic petting session? That would have been impossible. Laurie might flirt with me a little through eye contact and holding hands, but that's routine with any macho guy especially if he's partly Italian. With his beloved Caterina on his mind, he would obviously go no further.

'He did invite you to dress up and join the procession, and offered to lend you a very precious and ancient dress that's been handed down in his family. He has no young sisters, so it's yours for the wearing if you want it. I said I'd collect it, and then you can say if you want to wear it in a few days' time.'

'Why doesn't his wife wear it?' she asked suspiciously.

'She's too big. Guido thinks it would fit you very

well.' Laurie grinned. 'He was only measuring you for the dress when he eyed you from all angles.'

'So that's what he was doing?' she said drily. 'I felt like a prize pig being assessed for market.' She smiled. 'It was an evening of surprises. Which is your real name? Laurie Martin, so English and ordinary, or Lorenzo Martinello as he insisted on calling you?'

'If you were half English and half Italian you'd be confused too. I call myself Laurie for my work in England and among my English friends. I suppose I like to remember that my English mother, who died when I was quite small, always called me Laurie, but here I am as I was called at my christening— Lorenzo.'

'And what does Caterina call you?' she asked impulsively.

His eyes darkened. 'Caterina calls me Lorenzo, of course. She knows me as Italian. Her family and mine have been close for years.' He frowned. 'I've heard nothing since she left for Geneva.'

'That was only a few days ago. Can you expect a woman to write to anyone on her honeymoon?'

'You don't understand. I need to hear from her! I need to know that she's well.'

Samantha turned away, the bright sunlight mocking her heavy heart. He must be sick, to remain so involved with a woman he could never possess. What would her new husband think if he knew that Lorenzo Martinello was so besotted with Caterina that he expected to remain close to her even after her marriage?

She walked away from the terrace where they

were having coffee and refused Sarah's invitation to
swim. 'Later,' she said, wanting only to get on her
own and not to see the hurt in those dark blue eyes.
She fetched her bag and holdall and tugged at the
floppy linen hat so that her face was almost hidden
as she emerged into the bright sunlight.

'Wait.' Laurie was holding his car keys. 'It's too
hot to walk down that hill and even worse to walk
up with a basket of goods,' he said.

'You said exercise was good for me,' she replied.

'Not on a hot day like this one. I've told Mark
we'll get the food ready for the barbecue, and all
he'll have to do is to burn it for us.' He smiled, and
Samantha found she had to respond. His smile was
warm now and his attention on her as if he had
forgotten his broken heart. His hand on her bare
arm sent tiny tremors of exquisite feeling through
her entire body, and when he reached over in the
car to make sure that her door was locked she held
her breath, expecting him to sense that she was
trembling.

'I think he's more enthusiastic than skilled,' she
said. 'And I'd trust my own choice of steak rather
than his.'

'We could have lunch in Positano,' he suggested.
'Am I forgiven for Guido?'

The blue eyes laughed and Samantha shook her
head in mock reproach and said, 'How could anyone
forgive you for Guido?' but she found it easy to
forget that he was just asking her to lunch out of
polite concern for someone who had been of use to
him in a professional capacity.

'Have you got a credit card with you?' he asked.

She raised her eyebrows. 'How many steaks do you expect me to buy?'

'You don't buy any. I'll see to all that, but when we get to Positano, if you're at all like any girl I've taken there, you'll want to buy a dress or a shirt or something pretty. The shops are wonderful.'

'I don't know what to expect in Positano, but I'm content just to sit and look at the scenery,' she said half an hour later when they reached the coast and followed the winding road by the sweeping bays. White yachts that could be the holiday homes of wealthy film stars or world class businessmen sailed lazily across the horizon or swayed gently at inshore moorings, and the verdant terraces behind the villas were like bands of green silk holding the steep cliffs together. 'This is a wonderful place,' Samantha said, and sighed. 'I'd like to stay for months and just lose myself in sunshine and this marvellous sense of distance over the sea.'

'It could be arranged,' Laurie replied but when she glanced at the strong masculine profile she could read nothing to indicate that the arrangement would please him. 'This area's very rich, as is the land under Vesuvius where the molten lava fell and made the fields fertile. We have fruit and vines and olive trees. Vegetables like aubergines that we buy in England and pay high prices for quite small specimens grow like weeds and are a very common food in most Italian homes. We'll buy some and roast them in olive oil and basil,' he said. 'If Mark ruins the rest of the food, I can exist on vegetables quite happily.'

'How can you bear to leave Italy and live in London?' she asked.

'When I'm here, I enjoy life, but sooner or later I want to see red buses and hear the disciplined murmur of life at Beattie's.' He laughed. 'When I'm in London on a cold day with the gutters streaming and the sky grey then I long for Amalfi and the scent of herbs, but more and more I love England and the friends I've made there.' He looked sad for a moment. 'Many of my friends have moved away from here to America and other countries, and others have grown away from me.'

'Like Caterina?' she murmured.

His face was set in grim lines and he made no reply, but turned into a narrow side-street at the end of which was a broken wall revealing a crumbling terrace garden that made a level space to one side of the road.

'Is this Positano?' Disappointed, Samantha looked at the uninteresting side-street where Laurie parked the car under a tree.

'Not yet. It's quite close now, but this is where we walk. It's difficult to park down there and the few car parks are usually full just now, so I leave the car here and walk a hundred yards so that we can be free to move around. Come on, it's quite shaded with all these high walls and the villas perched up on the hill.'

They walked down to a wider road and turned a corner. Samantha gasped. Every building had a shop on the ground floor, and each one was filled with beautiful Italian dresses and suits and accessories. Laurie glanced at his wristwatch. 'Take your time. I have to meet someone,' he said. 'Do you see the hotel up there?' She shaded her eyes from the sun and saw a huge hotel, poised on the edge of the rock as if it might tumble down at any moment. 'We'll meet there at one o'clock,' he told her.

'I haven't a watch with me. How shall I know the time?'

He grinned. 'You'll know by the dirty looks you'll get if you stay in the shops after closing time at one, when the whole of Positano, except for the hotels and pizzerias, closes down for the entire afternoon, so if you want something, buy it, as we shall have gone from here before the place wakes up again.'

'I could do some window-shopping and come back here again on my own one day,' she said. 'Impulse buying isn't always successful.'

'Never leave anything you really want until later,' Laurie said slowly, his mood changing. He turned her towards him and his hands on her shoulders were firm and compelling. 'If you want something badly enough, take it when it offers,' he said softly, and kissed her cheek, then the corner of her mouth where her smile began, as if wanting to stay to become closer, then he drew away reluctantly, as if savouring a precious moment that must not be taken roughly but be left to be enjoyed later.

Samantha stared after him. He was in love with Caterina, and yet she knew that at that moment he wanted her as badly as she now wanted him. As she wandered down the road, hardly seeing the shops, a man smiled at her as if he wanted to stop and talk, but she hurried away, ignoring the come-on. This morning, the man who puzzled and excited her

really wasn't an English doctor, but was Lorenzo
Martinello, an Italian who could not pass by a pretty
girl without trying to chat her up or more; a man to
whom conquest was more important than love, and
charm was a dangerous weapon.

'Clothes,' she said as if just recalling why she was
there. 'Such clothes!' she murmured when she really
looked at them, and ten minutes later she was trying
on a beautiful confection of lace and silk that came
to her mid-calf and flowed like a zephyr as she
turned to look in the mirror at the muted greens and
pale coffee and gold that shifted and glowed with
every movement. A dress for a special occasion, a
fabulous dinner, or an important birthday cel-
ebration. She slid it from her shoulders and stepped
out of it, wondering if she would ever go to anything
that deserved such a dress.

'*Bellissima!*' the assistant said, and smiled, letting
the ripples of the skirt flow between her fingers. 'Not
expensive, and for you, *signorina*, a special offer.'
Samantha glanced at the price tag and did a quick
sum to change the Italian lire into sterling, but the
assistant was even quicker, using a pocket calculator,
and to her surprise the dress, although expensive,
was much less so than she'd imagined, and within
her budget.

Her smile made the girl know that she had a sale.
I might as well do as Laurie said and take what I
want when it offers, Samantha thought. If I came
back next week and the dress had been sold I'd be
mad at myself. I really do want it more than any
garment I've seen for a very long time. I can't have
the man I want, so why not buy something really

lovely to remind me of Italy and to wear when there's a party or they have a Christmas dance at Beattie's?

She glanced at other dresses in other windows, but dared not go into the shops or look too closely, as she dreaded seeing something even better, so she kept her attention on a shop with more ordinary holiday clothes. She bought a cotton T-shirt of bright blue with matching blue and white striped culottes, then decided to find the hotel before she did something quite mad, like buying a suede coat.

The terrace reached out over a deep chasm that cut through Positano on its way to the sea, and the view was breathtaking. A pink and white awning cast slabs of shade over the mosaic floor and the tables were set for lunch with spotless napkins and shining cutlery. Samantha glanced at the tables overlooking the view, but saw that they all had a reserved card on them. She hesitated, then walked to the edge of the balcony and looked down over the village. A distant clock struck the hour with the curiously cracked chime typical of many continental bells, and she wondered if Laurie was free of his business meeting.

Two figures were walking up the narrow main road and she put out a hand to wave, but Laurie was not looking up. The man with him talked earnestly and they seemed to be in a serious mood. At the turning to the hotel, they embraced and parted, and Laurie came quickly up the steps to the hotel, covering the ground with the lithe movements of a healthy male.

He saw Samantha standing there, uncertain where

to sit, and took her hand. 'My apologies, *cara*.' The affectionate address made her blush, even if it was probably the sort of greeting that men like him gave to any attractive female, and he seemed not to have noticed that he had used the expression. 'I reserved a table. Why didn't you ask for the one booked in my name?'

'You didn't say anything about it,' she said.

He shrugged and pulled back a chair for her at the best of the small tables for two by the balcony rail, and sat down in the opposite seat. Samantha smiled. Such arrogance let him take it for granted that he had been allotted the best as his right, with no reference to the waiter.

A small carafe of light white wine and a bottle of mineral water arrived quickly, and they sat and sipped the cold mixture while the food was prepared; tagliatelle, cooked *al dente* so it wasn't too soft and over-cooked, with a delicious sauce of tomatoes and basil, with garlic and onion and a generous helping of Parmesan cheese, freshly grated and left in a dish on the table with a large silver spoon.

Laurie was obviously dragging his mind back to her with a great effort. 'How did the shopping go?' he asked.

Samantha told him, and let him peep into the large carrier bag that held the lovely dress.

He glanced at the name on the side of the carrier and nodded approval. 'Beautiful colours, and the best shop here. Caterina gets most of her clothes there.'

'Caterina comes here?' she queried.

'This is her home,' he said. 'Her family have lived

here for centuries in a fine *casa* high above the town.
I came here to talk to her brother and to find out if
they have any news of her from Switzerland.'

The swirl of delicious pasta on her fork suddenly
lost its flavour. So that was why he had brought her
here, not for the enjoyment of her company but to
tear at his own heartstrings even more as he tried to
find news of the woman he couldn't forget and
couldn't erase from his life. The two men had talked
very seriously and with passion, as if Caterina's
brother agreed with Lorenzo Martinello that the
pretty woman had married the wrong man.

'People on honeymoon don't often leave messages
for relatives and friends,' she ventured.

'Honeymoon?' Laurie gave a short laugh. 'What
honeymoon?'

Samantha regarded him with some anxiety. He
was really flipping his lid!

'You know—a honeymoon! The time when two
people who are married and in love go away and
spend time together making love and enjoying each
other's company,' she replied sharply.

'I know what you mean, and I know it should be
a precious and wonderful experience, but Caterina
and her husband are quite different.'

'They're in love. I saw it clearly, and he just
couldn't take his eyes off her, so what's wrong?'

'Caterina's ill. Her husband is a wealthy business-
man who has a passion for healing by means of diet
and health foods and fringe medicine such as homoeopathy, and he refused to allow her to see a surgeon.' Laurie glanced up at the waiter who hovered
close by with the menu, then back at Samantha. 'She

should have married a doctor who would see that she has the care and attention she needs, but Paolo has a very forceful personality, and she accepted what he demanded even before they were married and thinks he can do no wrong.'

'*Signore*?' The waiter placed menus in front of them and suggested that the special Neapolitan ice-cream was good.

Laurie raised an enquiring eyebrow and Samantha nodded. 'For two, and coffee,' he ordered.

'Surely he'll see that she has the best attention?' Samantha queried. 'If he truly loves her he'll never put her health at risk. I know a very clever doctor who treats patients with homoeopathy and has excellent results. Maybe you're prejudiced, as so many conventional medics are when it comes to fringe medicine.' She looked at him and then away, hating his tense expression, but she wanted to shake him free of his obsession and make him face the fact that Caterina was married and there was nothing he could do to take her as his own wife, however much he was anxious about her health. She was obviously in good and loving hands, with wealth and influence to gain everything possible for her well-being.

Laurie moved restlessly and mashed his elegant ice-cream into a mess of pink and chocolate and white swirls. 'He insisted on taking her to Geneva to a very famous man who'll examine her, and she's promised to undergo his homoeopathic treatment if that's what he suggests.' He gave a short laugh. 'A wonderful honeymoon!'

'And if she doesn't respond to that or he finds he must ask for other opinions, what then?'

'This doctor does cure a lot of people with medical conditions,' Laurie admitted. 'But from the signs and symptoms I know she's a surgical case and no amount of his kind of drugs can touch it. He may realise this when he examines her and be wise and honest enough not to start any treatment until she's had another more conventional opinion, and if she shows no signs of improvement and they accept that a surgeon must be consulted, then they'll consult a surgeon over there in the normal way,' he admitted.

'It seems to me that she's in no danger,' Samantha said slowly. 'She has the best of both kinds of medicine ready to help her.'

'Caterina's brother made Paolo swear before the wedding ceremony that he'd take her to a surgeon if necessary, or he swore that he'd refuse to be Caterina's sponsor at the wedding, which would have caused her a lot of pain and humiliation.' Laurie slapped a hand on to the table-top and glared at Samantha as if she were responsible for all his worries. 'Time is of the essence,' he said. 'It may be a simple cyst on an ovary or it could be malignant, and in that case even a week or so of delay might make all the difference to her future.'

'You must love her very much,' Samantha said with a dry throat.

'Her family were as my own when my mother died,' he explained simply. He tried to smile, seeing her anxious face. 'More coffee? No? Then let's go to the clinic on the way back. You've not seen it yet, and we can check on Jenny. It seems that my diagnosis was correct. She does have toxic shock syndrome, and it's reacted quickly to the drugs I gave her.'

'*You* diagnosed?' Samantha looked up, flushed with annoyance, and her eyes were over-bright. How dared he accept all the kudos for what were her findings? 'If I'd said nothing you'd have had her on the operating table, looking for an acute appendix,' she said, then saw that he was laughing.

'I love you when your eyes glint green fire and that lovely bosom is a turbulent pillow of distress,' he said. 'No, I really meant to thank you, but you looked so miserable that I had to tease you. She's very much better, thanks to you, but you shall see for yourself.'

The town looked as if a spell had been cast over it, sending it to sleep and awaiting a signal to come to life again. 'This is the time to see the shops,' Samantha said, eyeing a jade and silver gown that was draped on a model in one window. 'I'm safe now, and I can look but not touch and certainly not buy.' A dog lay in the middle of the road as if he knew that everyone was resting and that any passing car would drive round him, and the hairpin bends were less hazardous, with little traffic.

'Is this it?' Samantha stared up at the dignified façade of an old piazza. 'It doesn't look much like a clinic,' she remarked.

Laurie drove round to the back of the building where the car park was half full and an ambulance stood empty by a wide glass door. The old house was as it had been for centuries, but behind it a new modern hospital block had been built, and it was into this entrance that they went. A pretty girl sat at a reception desk, and smiled when she saw Dr Lorenzo Martinello. They were taken up to a room on the first floor, and Samantha laughed when she saw Jenny, sitting out on a rattan couch with Mark, both of them absorbed in a game of Scrabble.

Mark started up and reddened. It was hardly the macho image that he wanted to display, and Samantha thought the couple looked like two children playing. 'Hi!' Jenny said, and looked very pleased to see them. 'They say I can go home to the UK in a day or so, or come back to the villa if they'll still have me at the language school.' She looked at Samantha as if she might have the power to tell her to stay in Italy.

'That can be arranged,' Laurie told her. 'Maria will be glad to feed you up, and there's no need to give up your course, so long as you do as the doctor here tells you and observe rigid hygiene.'

'Great!' Mark looked relieved. 'I'll see that she behaves,' he added, then saw the quizzical glance that Laurie gave him. 'I mean really behave,' he said, and Samantha knew that Jenny had been warned that sex would not be a good idea for a very long time.

'I have to have a test later to make sure that my Fallopian tubes aren't affected.' Jenny bit her lip. 'If they are, then I might not be able to have babies. I had no idea that being careless about hygiene could have such far-reaching effects.'

'You're young and healthy,' Laurie said. 'I doubt if there'll be any lasting complications, as this was an acute condition and hasn't been hanging about for months.'

Samantha told Mark that the barbecue was organised, and sympathised with Jenny, who was not quite well enough to join them. 'Never mind, Jenny,' she said. 'When you come back we'll give a party for you, if Sir Ralph doesn't object.'

Feeling that they weren't really needed to cheer up the patient as Mark had a very proprietorial air over her, Laurie took Samantha back to the villa. Guido was sitting on the terrace with a bottle of wine at his elbow. He grinned and produced a cardboard box and handed it to Samantha, then looked inside the carrier containing her new dress. He laughed and said something in very fast Italian that Samantha couldn't follow. Laurie turned red and cuffed Guido affectionately across the ear.

'What was that?' she asked suspiciously.

'Nothing,' he replied with annoying lightness. 'He wants you to try the dress on and come out for inspection.'

'He mentioned the other dress. The one I bought,' she persisted.

'Yes,' he agreed slowly as if choosing his words carefully. 'That's to wear afterwards when we go out on the town and enjoy the rest of the night.'

'I see. . . I think,' she said, and took both dresses into her room, more out of curiosity to see what dreadful costumes they had dreamed up a hundred years ago for the procession than with any intention of wearing it in public. The first layer of tissue paper came away, and she glimpsed scarlet and gold and felt the soft warmth of silk.

Carefully she unwrapped the garment—and caught her breath. A slim sheath of white silk, banded with scarlet velvet at and above the hem, became an underskirt for another layer that was cut away at one side. This was pale grey and gold with tiny motifs of the Cross of St Andrew in white and a neckline low enough to reveal her throat, but modestly fringed with scarlet bobbles and gold ribbon. A tiny veil of gold tissue completed the effect, and Samantha stood before the mirror with tears in her eyes. It was much more than fancy dress. It was the gown of a medieval lady, whose lover, a Templar Knight of the Cross of St Andrew, would lead her to the revels.

Shyly she ventured out into the sunlight and stood with downcast eyes by the balustrade of the terrace, almost hoping the two men would not turn round and see her. I can't wear it, she thought. They'll hate to see me in it as I'm not one of Guido's family and certainly not a relative of Lorenzo's.

As Guido turned, she was aware that at that moment she thought of Laurie as Lorenzo—completely Italian, as if she was being drawn into a charmed circle by wearing the dress.

'Ah! *Mamma mia!*' Guido exclaimed in an awed whisper. '*Si, signorina, si, si!*'

A pulse beat heavily in the throat of the doctor, who sat as if turned to stone. His eyes were dark as night and smouldered with a passion that made Samantha want to run away, or if he had held out his arms, to rush into them and beg him to take her away and make love to her, but he said nothing as he gazed at the dress and the girl in it, fixing the picture firmly in his memory for all time. Guido talked furiously, with an almost hysterical note, then calmed down, and, with an elegance that she had never suspected he could possess, took her hand reverently and kissed it, with no hint of lust but a kind of worship.

'What did he say?' she asked in a tight voice.

Laurie came out of a trance. 'He said that you're very beautiful and that the dress fits,' he said shortly.

'And the other? The bits I couldn't get for myself?'

'He said that the dress hasn't been worn for nearly twenty years as it fits no woman in his family and there's been no other to whom he would lend it.' He hesitated, then continued as if it must be said, 'He asks you to wear it in the procession because you're with me. He thinks we're lovers.'

'Tell him the truth,' she said in a small voice. Had Guido not heard that his Lorenzo Martinello was obsessed by Caterina? 'Tell him you're not in love with me and that we're here just because we happened to be here to see Sir Ralph.'

'I can't tell him that.' Laurie laughed without real humour. 'You can't spoil this for him, whatever your feelings are for me. Be my partner for the day and go back in time like the rest of Amalfi.'

'So you'll wear fancy dress too?' Keep it light, Samantha told herself. You wanted him to want you when he saw you in the dress, and his expression was only the sign of shock when he saw the dress worn by someone who suited it. Beware of your own wishful thinking.

'*Signorina*?' Guido's eyes begged for an answer.

'Tell him I'll do it, but you must instruct me, as I

know nothing about the history of the procession and may not do it well,' she said.

Guido kissed her on both cheeks and went away, talking to himself and forgetting the bottle of wine that he had hardly touched, and Samantha carefully changed out of the dress and hung it in her wardrobe beside the new modern one. She shivered slightly. The new dress gave her the same feeling, of an Italian era long ago, of elegance and passion, charm and violence, and she wondered if she could ever dare to wear it away from Italy. Deliberately she put on jeans and a rather sludgy-coloured shirt that hid her breasts in its ample folds and made her feel unobtrusive. She wandered out on to the terrace to the tray of tea that Maria had brought, and sat alone while Laurie and Nathan dragged the barbecue into the shelter of the wall and filled the base with charcoal.

'Pour me a cup,' Laurie called as if he had never seen the dress or the girl inside it. 'I'll just get this going as it takes an hour to be really ready, then I must see Guido again to fetch my gear.'

'Do we have a dress rehearsal?' asked Nathan with a grin.

'No, you do not! One day wearing that rig is quite enough, and I'm beginning to regret that I said I'd do it.'

'Why is that?' Samantha was curious to know what was embarrassing about wearing—what? A tabard or a long robe?

'Just think of yourself as a leading ballet dancer,' Nathan said with relish. 'Rather you than me, bud.'

'Tights?' Samantha laughed. 'Really tights? Like the ballet?'

'Cod-piece and all,' drawled Nathan.

'It isn't like that at all. I shall wear a long robe over the tights, with a cape and slashed sleeves and a skull-cap if I can get it to stay on.' Laurie sighed. 'June in Amalfi is hot, and yet they have to choose this time of the year for the procession. I shall be baked alive in all that gear.'

'You can take it off and parade in scarlet tights. Very butch,' Nathan said.

'Get that fire alight,' Laurie ordered. 'I want to forget it and enjoy a good steak tonight.' He eyed Samantha with amusement. 'Looks as if you want to put it out of your mind too. As you're dressed for action, go and pick some herbs from the plot by the kitchen. They make the meat taste good if we put them in the marinade, and the smell's out of this world when we burn them on the barbecue.' He sounded very businesslike, and Samantha knew he had forgotten the vision he had seen when she appeared in the gown. She crushed basil and sage between her fingers and closed her eyes. This was the scent of Italy, and she would remember it for ever.

CHAPTER FOUR

THE two Australians and four English students whom Mark had invited to the barbecue sat on the wall of the terrace eating garlic bread and drinking red wine. Samantha staggered out of the kitchen with the huge dish of steak, marinating in red wine, chopped onion and olive oil, with crushed basil and tomato purée. Nathan flung a handful of herbs on to the white-hot coals and the smell drifted over the terrace, then he took the heavy dish from her.

'Thanks,' she gasped, 'I nearly dropped it. We've far too much food, and Maria will go mad if we leave huge amounts of cooked steaks in her fridge.'

He grinned. 'Never heard of doggy bags? There won't be a scrap left if those scavengers take what's left back to the hostel. You mix the salad and I'll get these on the fire.'

'Where's Mark?' she asked.

'He's bringing paper plates and more wine, and Laurie's cooking a dish of aubergines in the kitchen.' Nathan laughed and stuck a long fork into a steak, transferring it to the barbecue and watching the coals sizzle as the olive oil dripped through the grid on to the fire. He added enough to cover the grid and stood back as Mark appeared ready to take over. 'It's all yours,' Nathan said. 'C'mon, Sam, let's get sloshed.' He tried to take her hand, but she backed away.

Samantha laughed. 'Nobody calls me Sam,' she protested. 'I hate it.'

'Have some wine,' he said. 'Whatever they call you, drink with me and say you love me.'

She backed away. 'I'll get the rest of the garlic bread,' she said, and ran into the kitchen.

'House on fire, or just Mark sending up smoke signals?' asked Laurie, smiling.

'I came for the rest of the bread,' she said in a subdued voice.

'Nearly ready, and I'll come with you and bring the baked aubergines.' He put down the cloth he was holding and took her hand. 'What's wrong?'

'Nothing.' She shrugged. 'I think Nathan sampled the wine before the others arrived and he's a bit high. It's nothing,' she assured him as she saw his mouth tighten. 'Just Nathan being a bit over the top.'

'I'll come out and see what's happening,' he said.

'No need,' she assured him calmly. 'I can handle him. He's quite happy and not really bothering anyone yet, but he might get stroppy later.' She frowned. 'He can make a pass at me and I can laugh it off, but one of the female students is all wide-eyed and ready for adventure and very vulnerable, and he does have a certain attraction.'

'These are done,' Laurie said, and took the large tray of sizzling vegetables from the oven. Samantha followed him with two large loaves, sliced and spread with garlic butter, wrapped in foil and hot from the oven.

The steaks were doing nicely and Mark was in his element. He wore a large apron that belonged to

Maria and was playing Italian opera on tape to make a background. 'Pity Jenny couldn't come,' he said. 'But I promised I'd take her to Ravello to a hotel where they have a barbecue once a week. Not as good as this, but not bad,' he conceded.

Nathan was drinking again and now turned his attention to the pretty blonde girl from Eastbourne, who Samantha suspected had led a very sheltered life before going away to the language course with a schoolfriend. She was flushed and happy, as Nathan showed that he was attracted to her. She held out her glass for more wine, and Samantha suggested she should eat some garlic bread. She served her first with steak to mop up the alcohol and gave a sigh of relief when everyone, including Nathan, was busy eating.

Laurie made sure that everyone ate well and suggested mineral water as a thirst-quencher after all the food, and most of the party took his advice, but Nathan continued to drink the heady local wine and pressed more and more on the now slightly confused girl.

'Rhoda, have some fruit,' Samantha suggested, and saw the girl put down her glass. She picked it up and took it away, substituting a glass of Coke, and when she sipped it Rhoda showed no sign that she noticed the change.

Nathan caught Samantha by the arm as she went round with the bowl of fruit, and in a hoarse whisper asked her to dance. She saw that his eyes were reddened and his speech was slurred. 'Later,' she said, smiling. 'Help Mark take the rest of the food into the kitchen and put it in a plastic box for the

students. You said they'd like to take it home,' she
added as he frowned. 'That was a very good idea of
yours, Nathan, and I know they'll be glad to have
it.'

He gave a fatuous grin as if proud of himself and
wandered off into the house to fetch the box.
'Everything all right?' Laurie appeared at her elbow.

'Fine,' she said. 'That is, I hope so, but he drove
up here and brought some of the students with him,
and now he has a car and a very inflated ego and has
drunk far too much wine.' In the distance they heard
the steady, subdued roar of traffic down on the main
road, hidden from sight and almost quiet from this
distance, but they knew that the roads were busy
even at night and that a driver needed all his faculties
to cope with it.

'He can't drive tonight,' Laurie said firmly. 'Since
he went to sleep at the hostel he's been up here a
lot, but never when he's drunk. I'll take his car keys
if they're in the ignition, and he'll think he's mislaid
them and walk down the hill.'

'I'll tell the others that he's not giving lifts tonight
so they should make their own way back when they
feel they've had enough here,' she said. 'The only
danger might be if some of them wanted a lift down
to the village to the one place where there's music
until very late.'

She watched Laurie go into the car park by the
side of the house, and experienced a feeling of deep
friendship that was something apart from love. We
could be so good together, she thought, but only if
friendship was matched with love. She sighed,

admitting to herself that friendship would never be enough, unless she settled for second best in his life.

They shared many interests and their professions interlocked closely. Was it possible to work with him, just to be near to him, even if he could never love her? Many women adored colleagues or employers for years without being loved in return, but they had some satisfaction in knowing that each day they could see and hear their beloved and maybe share any affection left over from his family and real loves.

Samantha shook herself. Maudlin thoughts about a man who could never love her led to nothing but depression and unhappiness, and she knew she could never be satisfied with half a love.

'It's no use. He has the keys and he's getting upset because nobody will drive with him.' Laurie looked serious. 'I'll get my car from the garage by the annexe, and you tell him I'll drive him home and he can collect his car in the morning. On no account must anyone get into his car with him tonight.'

Samantha went back to the barbecue and looked around through the blue smoke-filled air. The fire was reduced to pale ashes, and the smell of burned bread and the remains of food from the plates that someone had thrown on the fire was pungent on the night breeze. Someone had spilled a bottle of wine on the terrace, and that too made the air rank. She shivered. The party spirit had gone and it now seemed more like a wake. She called, but Mark had vanished and so had most of the party. Of Nathan there was no sign, and to her horror she heard his car start up, and thought she heard a girl laughing, or was she screaming?

Laurie's car appeared from the driveway to the cottage and she dragged open the door. 'He's gone,' she said. 'I think he's taken Rhoda with him, but I'm not sure about the others. Oh, there's Mark. Thank God he's still here, and Sarah went to bed early with a headache from too much sun, so she's safe.'

'Get in!' Laurie drove down the track from the house, and slowed down when he saw three of the students walking down. 'Did Nathan drive down?' he called.

'Going like the clappers with only his parking lights on,' said one boy. 'Rhoda's with him, but she didn't really want to go.'

'Couldn't you stop him?'

'Sure, if I wanted my head split! He's bigger than me and mean with it tonight. He hit Bruce and made his nose bleed, then he grabbed Rhoda and ran off.'

Laurie let in the clutch and slowly drove down towards the main road. 'We can't stop him now, and the last thing we need is Nathan thinking we're making a race of it! But we might have to pick up the pieces,' he muttered.

In daylight, the road had been just another picturesque but winding road that opened up fine views and gave a sense of adventure, but now, under the dark sky, each bend took on a more sinister aspect, and Samantha was reminded of a corner on the Naples road where two wrecked cars had been left as a warning to other careless drivers. Twice they caught a glimpse of red rear lights, but they had no way of knowing if the car in front was Nathan's.

'If he takes the side-road to the hostel he might make it,' Laurie said grimly, 'but if he misses the turning he'll have to go by the main road further down and take a loop back, and that's busy.'

'Can't we try to catch up and shout to him to stop?' she asked.

'No. In his condition he'll think we're just having fun and he'll drive even faster.' He swore in Italian as a car came up the hill and the driver leaned out of the open window to shout a warning to Laurie.

'What did he say?' asked Samantha.

'Only that a maniac's driving down there with dim side-lights and no sense of speed, going from side to side on the road and only just missing obstacles.' Laurie quickened speed but stayed well behind the car in front, which now could easily be recognised.

'That's the turning to the hostel,' Samantha said. 'He's going on!'

The road took a sharp turn and they lost the car from view. 'Well, he managed that turning without incident,' Laurie said. 'Let's hope he can manage the next. That's the one that worries me.'

'Is it bad?' she asked, her eyes wide with fear.

'There's a drop down to a neglected vineyard as the fence has been broken for weeks, and the last accident there destroyed the lamp over the turn in the road. There's no warning except for an unlit sign.'

He dropped speed and eased the car round the next bend, keeping well to his own side of the road, and Samantha stared at the strong hands on the

wheel. They were as flexible as fine steel; hands that
could drive with perfect discipline, yet they were
hands that could touch the silk of a medieval dress
with sensitivity, conscious of its beauty and fragility,
and hands that could send a wave of desire through
a woman's body, at their slightest touch.

She looked ahead, her silent horror making her
cold. They both heard the crash, and Laurie drew in
to the side of the road and switched on his hazard
lights to make sure that other drivers saw the car.
Samantha followed him over the rough, stone-
strewn verge to the spot where the car had ploughed
through the weeds and what had been left of the
hedge.

'Stay back,' he ordered, but she followed him.
'*No!*' he insisted. 'Not until I've looked down there.'

'You forget I'm a nurse,' she retorted, suddenly
angry that he should think her just a helpless female
who might faint at the sight of an accident.

'As if I could forget that,' he replied with a short
laugh. 'But I think I can diagnose this one. There's
a flashlight in the glove compartment and another in
the trunk,' he said. 'Fetch them both. It's so damned
dark!'

The car lights down below glowed dimly through
the thick undergrowth, and Samantha picked her
way carefully over roots and loose earth to join
Laurie at the bottom of the fall. He took the largest
lamp without speaking and shone it on the wrecked
car. One door was open, almost wrenched from its
hinges, and the vehicle was partly on its side.

A groan made her swing round and shine her
torch on to a torn bush. 'Rhoda!' she exclaimed, and

pulled aside the branches. Rhoda lay on her stomach, but was already trying to turn and sit up.

'Move very slowly, and only if it doesn't hurt,' Samantha ordered.

'I think I'm all right,' Rhoda said. 'Bruised, and I think there's blood on my leg. My jeans are sticky, but I can walk.' She glanced up at the side of the terrace where the car had come over, and shuddered. 'I don't think I can climb that,' she admitted.

'Sit there and I'll see where the real entrance is,' Samantha told her. 'Workmen and farmers must come in here by a gate on the level, and it may be over there.'

'Is Nathan OK?'

'Laurie's with him,' Samantha said cautiously. 'My concern is you.' She walked along the path and found a gate that led to the road and the lanes to the other levels of the vine terraces. 'Rhoda,' she called, and helped the girl to walk along to the gate. 'Stay there until we bring the car,' she suggested. 'Sit on that log and I'll go and help Laurie.'

The lamp was propped up on a root and Laurie was struggling to wedge a log under the car so that he could open the driver's door. Samantha added her efforts to his, and eventually, after much panting and shoving, the car eased back. Nathan was unconscious, and as the door opened his limp form slid from behind the wheel and Laurie let him slide to the ground as gently as possible. Quickly he turned off the ignition as there was a strong smell of petrol, and together they lifted Nathan clear of the car and along the lane towards the road.

'All wrong!' Laurie said. 'But we can't do this

according to the book. Ideally we should put a collar on him before moving him at all, in case he has a whiplash injury of his upper neck and spine when the car hit the floor, but now I'm more worried about the leaking tank and making sure he gets out of this alive.' He glanced at his watch in the light of the torch that Samantha had strung round her neck on its cord. 'He's been unconscious for seven minutes,' he said, and stated the time.

'Only seven minutes? It seems like forever.' She pulled the cord over her head. 'You'd better have this torch now. When I get back home I'll buy one like this for the car. Very useful in an emergency, and in the dark it's too easy to put it down and lose it. I switched it off for a second back there and would never have found it if I'd put it on the ground. You'll need this one to find the bigger one. It seems to be switched off.'

'I dropped it and it went out. I'll find it and shine it up towards the road so that people know where we are.' He listened. 'I can hear voices now.' He shouted for help and an ambulance, in Italian and English, and Samantha took the torch again.

'You stay with Nathan. He's stirring slightly, and you can tell the people up there what you need. I'll find your torch,' she said.

She walked slowly as the ground was very uneven, and suddenly heard Laurie call her name. It was a cry of agony, of such horror that she paused and half turned, thinking he was somehow injured, or that Nathan was dying or was disorientated and fighting the doctor who was caring for him.

In that split second she saw what Laurie had

seen—the lighted cigarette end flying up in a careless arc high above the bushes on the edge of the terrace and with almost slow motion coming down into the scene of the accident.

Samantha turned back towards Laurie, and stumbled. In another second she was seized in a powerful embrace that had no hint of tenderness but was wonderfully reassuring as he dragged her unceremoniously along the path, then flung her to the ground and hid her body with his own as the blast of the ignited petrol went up like a bomb. '*Mia cara*!' she heard dimly, then fragments of blazing wood showered over them and a cry from above told them the rescuing party feared the worst.

Men ran from the gate as Rhoda pointed the way and a stretcher was placed on the ground beside Nathan, then the men took him to the waiting ambulance. 'Are you all right?' Laurie asked anxiously.

'Yes, just winded,' Samantha said, and coughed as the smoke found her lungs. 'What about you?'

He tore the shirt from his back and she saw that it was smouldering, the cotton in holes where the ashes had burned a way through. He beat out the remains of the fire, and Samantha saw that red patches were forming on the smooth brown skin. 'Stay there,' she ordered, and ran along to the gate and up the path to the car. A bottle of mineral water that she had noticed was still there, and she hurried back with it.

'Put the shirt on,' she said quickly. 'I'll pour water over it to contain the burn and lessen the pain.' He did as she suggested, and shivered as the cold water soaked the shirt, then he relaxed as the first discomfort abated.

'*Mia cara*,' he said softly, 'that's so good.' He took her in his arms and kissed her, slowly and with deep passion, until she wondered if she would dissolve into a cloud of ecstasy. Her hands stole up behind his head and neck, and she forgot that he was in love with Caterina and knew only that they were together in a close embrace and that he wanted her.

'Ouch!' Laurie drew away, and Samantha fell back as he released her. 'You missed a bit on my neck,' he said ruefully. She saw his white teeth gleam in the glow that came from the burned-out car, and he laughed.

'We'd better get back and I'll dress your burns,' she said shakily. This is madness, she told herself. He kissed me because we'd been through a bad experience together and he thought I needed comfort. Maybe he needed comfort! What does it matter? He kissed me, but it's nothing to him. One moment he was saving my life, and then the next he was breaking my heart.

She poured the rest of the water over the back of his neck and took a delight in seeing that this time he didn't enjoy it.

'Don't fuss. I can drive,' Laurie said.

'Have you dressings for burns at the villa?' she asked, and settled a now tearful Rhoda, who was suffering from a mild degree of delayed shock, in the back of the car.

'Enough,' he replied shortly, sounding cross.

'Was it something I said?' she asked with a tinge of irony.

'I'm sorry, I really am, if I seem bad-tempered, but I can imagine what the next few hours will be like. Papers and forms and more papers and interviews with the police. Thank God that Nathan was staying at the hostel, which means that Sir Ralph won't be involved with the authorities. Just us lucky ones who happened to be with him at the barbecue, where nothing unlawful happened, but, unfortunately for us, we were the ones who found him.'

'Fortunately for Nathan,' Samantha said firmly. 'He'd be dead inside that burned-out car if you hadn't dragged him clear.' For a second she rested a hand on his arm. 'You saved me too,' she said. 'If you hadn't shouted, I'd have been close enough to have been badly burned. I shall be grateful for that for ever.'

'How grateful?' he asked. 'I'm not sure I encourage gratitude. It might colour your true feelings. Gratitude often does that, so I shall never know if you meant that kiss or if you responded in a fit of thankfulness.' He smiled. 'Whatever the reason, I treasure the memory, that is until you poured cold water over me again. Was that to cool my ardour?'

'Of course not,' she said, then blushed. 'I mean, I knew you were burning and needed cooling. . .no, that's not it,' she amended, embarrassed. 'You know what I mean!'

'I hope so.' Laurie stopped the car by the main entrance to the villa, and as he got out he was limping slightly.

'Rhoda, you must sleep in the villa tonight so that we can keep an eye on you,' Samantha said. 'Feeling OK? No bones broken?' she asked in a bracing voice, and Rhoda stopped crying. 'Good. Run a bath in my bathroom—not hot, not cold, and put lots of salt in it,' she said. In the light from the hall lamps, she saw that the back of Laurie's jeans was peppered with small holes with burned edges. 'You didn't mention that there were other burns,' she said accusingly.

'I'd had enough of cold water poured over me, and I didn't want to be drowned,' he replied with feeling. 'These are very minor and they'll be fine with a touch of burn cream on them.'

'First, saline and careful drying, and I'll see what dressings you have that I can use. We may get away with dry dressings if the skin hasn't blistered,' she said. 'I think I caught it before the blisters had time to form.'

'Is this the shock treatment they teach you at Beattie's?' He pulled the wet fabric away from his skin and eased the shirt over his head with Samantha's help.

'It seldom fails if done promptly. In the operating theatre, one of the sisters makes sure there's a huge deep jug of sterile saline ready before each case, and if someone has scalded an arm in the sterilising-room by a gush of hot steam as a lid to a steriliser is opened, she makes her or him plunge the whole arm into the saline and keep it there for a full minute. Unless there's any delay, the blisters never form and the pain disappears. When I have my own theatre, I shall do that,' she added.

'You're the bossiest woman I've ever met,' he told her with a hint of real irritation. 'I suppose now you think you have to bath me?' He blushed. 'Nobody's

done that since I was seven when I broke my arm,'
he recalled.

'Only your back,' she replied demurely, but her
lips twitched with delight at the thought that she
could make this charismatic, macho male feel at a
loss. 'Just imagine me in a white cap and duty coat
and you won't feel embarrassed.'

'She's a nurse, she's a nurse, she's a nurse,' he
muttered as she led the way to the bathroom.

Samantha tested the water and held out her hand
for the keys to the medicine cupboard. 'A nice long
soak for at least ten minutes, and then I'll come and
dress the worst of them.' She turned at the door.
'Want any help? Are your jeans stuck down?'

'I can manage,' he said through gritted teeth.
'You're enjoying this, woman! Are all nurses sadists
like you?'

'Only the best,' she replied sweetly. 'Only the
ones who can nurse without becoming emotionally
involved with patients and so give their best service.'

'What happened to gratitude?' he called.

'You said you didn't want any,' she murmured as
she went away to prepare the dressings. 'Put a kettle
to boil,' she said to Rhoda, who was wandering
about as if in a trance.

'I don't know what to do,' the girl said. 'I ought
to be with him!' she announced with a fine show of
drama.

'With who?' Samantha asked.

'Nathan. I feel it's my fault. He wanted to take
me dancing.' Rhoda blushed. 'He told me he loved
me,' she added with a kind of disbelieving pride.

'Nathan loves everybody,' Samantha replied,

twirling a plastic glove to fill it with air. She held the glove to her cheek, but there were no leaks of air, so she put it on and washed her gloved hand in water heavily laced with mild antiseptic, the best she could do without sterile gloves. She consoled herself by thinking that gloves weren't vital to the dressings as the skin on Laurie's back was not broken, but she suspected that she was trying to make some sort of barrier between them when she had to touch him.

Resolutely she tore off the glove. He was just a patient in Casualty with minor burns. If she held on to that thought, any personal feelings would never arise. 'What if he wakes up and I'm not there?' Rhoda asked, in a little-girl voice.

'Nathan was far too drunk to know what he did tonight, so try not to think about anything he said or did, Rhoda. He told you he loved you, he told me he loved me, and no doubt he told every female at the party the same, but you were the one who sat with him and drank with him and went with him in that car.' Samantha smiled sympathetically. 'He's very attractive, but a bit of a womaniser, Rhoda, and I advise you to go easy with him for a while.'

'You're jealous.' The girl's eyes flashed and her bottom lip quivered again as if more tears were coming. She followed Samantha back to the kitchen where a space had been cleared on the huge table for the dressings and lotions. 'You can't believe that any man would rather have me than you, can you? He said you were frigid and not his type. He told me that!' she added as if Nathan had the monopoly on truth.

'Make coffee,' Samantha said in a tired voice. 'I

have work to do, but we'll wait for half an hour until they've decided what's wrong with Nathan, then telephone, if that's what you'd like?'

Rhoda looked at the neat tray containing scissors and gauze, the tin of fine net soaked in petroleum jelly and Balsam of Peru, strapping and a small bottle of acriflavine solution, and her mood changed. 'I think I'd like to be a nurse,' she said. 'Maybe if I find I don't like college, I could do my training. I'll bring the coffee as soon as it's ready,' she added in a more subdued tone.

'Thanks,' Samantha said, and took the tray into the bathroom, where a day bed in one corner of the huge old-fashioned room would be fine as a casualty couch.

From the depths of the bath, Laurie viewed her with apprehension and looked with longing at the bathrobe hanging behind the door at least three yards away from the bath. He saw her put thick towels on the couch and turn to the small table on which she had put the tray. 'I feel fine,' he began. 'The salt water has worked wonders and I shall be all right when I'm dry.' He slid further down in the water. 'Maybe I'll soak for a while longer,' he suggested. 'Put a towel on that stool close to the bath and I'll manage.'

'Come now, Dottore Lorenzo Martinello, we can't have that! At least one small burn will need tulle gras if it's to heal without a scar and isn't to stick, and I must inspect the others that you can't see for yourself.' Samantha smiled kindly. 'I'll try not to hurt you. Do the Italians have a lower pain threshold than the Brits? In that case concentrate on being Dr

Martin and keep a stiff upper lip, and you may feel better.'

She patted the couch invitingly. 'Come on,' she pleaded in her best children's ward staff nurse voice. 'I'm really quite gentle.'

'I'll bet you are,' he muttered. 'That's the least of my worries. I'll catch my death of cold if I have to walk naked across that tiled floor. And you'd die of fright. Throw me a towel! Nurse Samantha Croft, you are a very efficient, very pretty and quite heartless bitch!'

'I love you too,' she murmured, and held out a huge fluffy bath sheet, which he snatched and draped firmly round his middle like a sarong. Water dripped from his brown legs and he seemed to tower above her as he paused as if to say something even more biting before climbing on to the couch, face down.

'Right.' His relief was evident. 'The one on the shoulder is sore, but the others are fine.'

Gently Samantha patted the skin over his shoulders dry and inspected the damage. His back was smooth and firm and the muscles that flinched when she touched a tender place were finely moulded but not as heavily obvious as those of a lifeguard or fitness freak. 'One real dressing and a few dabs of acriflavine ointment on the red patches, then a few dabs of aqueous flavine on the minor ones to keep them clean,' she said. Swiftly and with great care she put actions to words, and he sighed as the cool, lubricated gauze covered the one really sore spot and was expertly strapped into place under a light gauze swab.

He moved slightly as if he was ready to get up.

'Thank you,' he said dismissively, but she dabbed a little more flavine close to the shrouding towel, then pulled it down to reveal the cleft of his buttocks.

'I thought so,' she said, and put more bright orange flavine on another piece of cotton wool and dabbed again. She found a small burn that needed a patch of dressing just below the triangle of dimples that she had learned were the accepted guide to mark the site of the fifth lumbar vertebra. Absent-mindedly she dabbed a hint of orange dye on each dimple, and giggled.

'What are you doing?' Laurie asked impatiently.

'I could do a perfect lumbar puncture,' she said. 'You have lovely dimples.'

'Have you *quite finished*?' His voice sounded dangerous.

'No!' Suddenly she was aware of his body, not as a patient but as a normal, active, heterosexual male. Her courage failed as she backed away, afraid of further contact. 'Yes, it's all done. You can do any abrasions on your front.'

'Thank God for that!' His relief was comic, and she relaxed.

Rhoda came in with a coffee-tray and eyed the half-naked man with amusement. 'Measles?' she asked. 'Can I have some to paint my boobs when I go topless?'

'Have you ever?' Laurie asked, with a laugh.

'Well, no, not exactly,' she replied, suddenly shy. 'Sarah said she would if I would, but we haven't done it yet. The beach is too crowded and I don't know if it's allowed there, and here by the pool—

well, with people I'll meet at the next lecture, it's embarrassing.'

'Take Nurse Croft with you as a chaperon. No man would dare to chat you up if she was there to protect you. She scares the living daylights out of me,' he added with fervour. 'Hand me that bathrobe,' he ordered. 'Now, drink your coffee and we'll ring the hospital in Naples where Nathan was taken and find out how he is.' He flexed his shoulders and smiled at Samantha. 'Apart from the trauma of being at your mercy, full marks. I can't feel a thing.' He sipped the hot dark coffee and eyed her over the top of the mug, secure now in the enveloping bathrobe. 'Did anyone ever tell you what sexy hands you have, Nurse Samantha Croft?'

CHAPTER FIVE

SAMANTHA put down the large coffee-cup and regarded Laurie with amused interest. 'Did you sleep well?' she asked.

'Thanks to you, yes. The spot on the shoulder's a bit sore, but the rest is fine.' He eyed her with suspicion. 'Were all those dabs of red really necessary? I examined my back in the long mirror in Sir Ralph's room, and I'm as spotty as a leopard, even in places where it doesn't hurt.'

'I'm only a nurse,' she replied demurely. 'I had to be quite sure that I'd covered all eventualities.' But her smile made him look even more put out. 'When Sir Ralph arrives I don't want him saying I've lost my touch.'

A gleam of the dark blue eyes showed an emotion other than annoyance, and it made her look away. 'Ah, yes, that touch,' he said. 'I can assure Sir Ralph that you have a very special touch. Ever thought of taking up relaxing massage?' He saw her faint blush and grinned. 'When do you want me for the next treatment, Nurse Croft?'

'Can't you manage now?' she queried.

'Not the shoulder burn. I think it needs a fresh dressing. Shall we say in half an hour, after I've had breakfast? I need some gentle treatment.'

She nodded, then made an effort to sound normal. 'Have you rung the hospital this morning?'

'Yes. Nathan has had a few X-rays taken which show no fractures, and he's reacting to all the routine tests that would show up brain damage or loss of motor or sensory nerve function. He had a few cuts stitched, but no plaster casts were necessary, so he'll be walking today, if his stiff leg responds to physio. I'll visit him later and see that he has everything he needs, but of course the police have been talking to him, and he's very depressed and angry with himself for getting into that state.'

'I think I'll visit him too,' Samantha said. 'I feel rather sorry for him, even if it was his own fault and he could have injured Rhoda.'

'I spoke to him on the phone and he did ask if you were very angry with him,' Laurie admitted. 'That seemed to worry him.' His eyes were hooded and his mouth set in a firm line. 'Don't feel too sorry for him,' he said.

'Why not? Aren't we trained to show a little compassion and to give a large helping of tender loving care?' Her eyes sparkled. Dr Laurie Martin was not pleased to think that she could spare any tender loving care for Nathan. If she didn't know better, she could imagine he was being slightly possessive, almost jealous.

'That's different,' he retorted. 'I hope they added *objective* compassion when they taught you so well.'

'That's what I mean,' she said quietly. 'All my work is purely professional.'

'Then put on your mental uniform and come with me,' he said, and pushed his empty plate away.

The small burn was clean and healing well, as it was not deep. The circle of gauze that covered it was

easily hidden under an adhesive plaster in which
Samantha had cut small pin-holes to allow air to
penetrate and so prevent the skin from becoming
soggy. She touched one or two orangy red spots with
fresh flavine, but most of his back was clear. 'Would
you like me to wash away all the dye that isn't
needed?' she asked, as she would do for any patient.

'Please,' he said. 'If I'm to swim again when the
shoulder's cleared up I can't go down looking as if I
have the orange plague.'

Samantha bit her lip. She recalled a case on the
skin ward at Beattie's when she, as a junior nurse,
had been detailed to wash off gentian violet dye that
stained the skin bright purple. It had not been a
great success. The purple had faded to dim grey
patches that were even less attractive. She fetched a
bowl of water and a face cloth, some soap and a
small bottle of fragrant hair shampoo, which as a
very mild detergent might have a good chance of
removing a stain without being harsh.

Laurie lay quite still while she worked, taking her
time as the stains were stubborn, her hands moving
rhythmically over the firm muscles, almost massag-
ing his back as she washed away the dye, and she
took a sensual pleasure in the close physical contact.
He relaxed at first and then became tense, his
breathing uneven his hands clenched spasmodically
at his sides. 'Enough,' he said in a strangled voice.

'I haven't finished,' she said, surprised at his
vehemence. 'I was being as gentle as I could, but
some of the marks will have to stay.'

'Fine. I can live with them,' he said firmly. 'Go
away.' He buried his head in the pillow and stayed

face down on the couch. 'Lord,' she heard him murmur, 'I never knew what patients had to suffer until now.'

'I didn't hurt you,' she protested indignantly.

'No! You were as gentle as a harem girl with fine scented oils designed to make men mad. As I said, you have. . .healing hands.'

'That's not what you said. Oh!' She blushed scarlet and picked up the bowl of water and hurried from the room, leaving him to dry himself and to ease the shirt over his sore shoulder, and when she went back to take away the dressing tray he was sitting on the side of the bed, looking flushed but normal.

'Thanks,' he said.

'All better?' she asked.

'No, I wouldn't say better, but that can't be helped here,' he said enigmatically. 'I'll drive you in to visit Nathan and you can do some shopping if you like before we get back here.'

'Fine.' She avoided eye contact and tidied the room, folding the wet towels neatly and putting back the top on the shampoo bottle. 'You think you'll be able to dress up for the procession? If not, I think I'll call it off too. I'm not Italian, and they might resent a stranger wearing that lovely gown.'

'Don't think that. Were you upset when Guido assumed that we were lovers? As such you're not a stranger but very welcome.' His eyes forced her to answer him as if he really needed to know.

'It isn't that.' She moved restlessly, unable to forget that Caterina was his one and only love. 'You must have been a bit embarrassed too.'

'Why? It's a compliment for any man to be

assumed to be the lover of a beautiful girl—but I was forgetting. You nurse men, not love them, and you give only professional tender loving care and forget that it can have a deep and lasting effect on a patient. Promise me one thing?'

'What?' she asked.

'Keep away from Nathan. He'd take advantage of that care, that. . .touch.'

'He doesn't have orange spots on his back, so I'm not likely to make any physical contact with him, and I'm immune to men like him,' she assured him.

'Immune to all men? Have you never been in love?'

'I have dates and men find me attractive,' she said, avoiding a straight reply. 'It isn't always possible to make a life with the one person you love.' Her mouth was dry and she shivered. How could he know the tension she had been under ever since he came to the villa, knowing that he was in love with Caterina?

'No, I suppose not.' He looked sad. 'Let's go and see Nathan. Do you think Rhoda would want to come too?' Samantha had a fleeting suspicion that Laurie wanted Rhoda to go with them so that he could avoid being alone with her.

'I could ask,' she said. 'But do you think it wise? She shed enough tears last night and seems to think she should have been at Nathan's bedside when he woke up. In his state he might say "Who are you?" as I'm sure he would have been the same at the barbecue with any girl unfortunate enough to catch his attention when he was drunk and amorous.'

'Including you?'

'He tried,' she said crisply. 'I just backed away politely. I can handle that kind of situation. Would you believe that even patients get a bit amorous when all I do is care for them in the usual way?'

'I can believe it,' Laurie said with feeling. 'Wear that disgusting hat. It hides your face and will protect you from all men,' he added. 'We'll buy him some grapes and chocolate.'

They drove carefully past the gap in the hedge which had now been taped off by the police, and in daylight it looked even worse than they'd imagined.

Mark had begged a lift as far as the village near the clinic, and he stared in horror as he thought of what had happened last night. 'Dad complained about this corner last year, and they've done nothing but put up a very dodgy fence,' he told them. 'By the way, he's expected tonight, so he'll be in time for the celebrations.'

'Great!' Laurie said. 'We can combine business with pleasure. Will you let the manager of the clinic know that Sir Ralph will be in touch tomorrow? They know which patients he wants to see there, and will make all the arrangements. I'm glad he's ready to work here, as I must get away soon. I took a short leave, but I have commitments in London, and other places.'

Samantha said nothing. He was going away, and when she next saw him it might be in a busy ward at Beattie's or just passing by in the corridor when she went about the hospital. A crisp uniform and a flapping white coat would pass each other in an almost completely negative way, the magic of Amalfi would die and she had nothing to take its place. A few more weeks in this paradise could be full of light and warmth if he was there, but in a villa with people she hardly knew it would be cold and boring.

How could one man make all that difference? She had bundles of pamphlets with details of boat trips and visits to famous landmarks, including the volcano Vesuvius, and she had been excited when she first realised that she would visit Pompeii. Before Laurie arrived in her life she would have enjoyed all this. Now she saw only the empty days ahead.

'Do you think Sir Ralph might be glad of my help?' she asked, after Mark had left them, carrying a bag of clean clothes for Jenny.

'No, you're here as a convalescent,' he replied. 'He suggested this break to prepare you for work at Beattie's, and you must get really fit before you return to London.' She glanced at his face quickly and saw that he was smiling wickedly. 'You have one patient who needs all your exclusive care and treatment. More work would exhaust you.'

'I don't like one-to-one nursing. That's why I opted for theatre work next when I have my certificate, and not private nursing.' She lowered her eyelids.

'You find one patient at a time, like me, boring?' His question came sharply, and she saw that he was annoyed.

'Yes—I mean no. You aren't a patient,' she said. 'I mean—that is—you're not boring, but when I nurse private patients. . .' Her voice trailed away.

'You'd rather I went to the clinic for any further dressings? Maybe I should. I'm working you much too hard for a convalescent who has nothing to do but lie in the sun, eat and do a little gentle sightseeing.'

'That's not fair.' Tears filled her eyes and she groped for a tissue in the depths of her bag. 'I enjoyed treating your burns.'

'So did I, in a masochistic way,' Laurie said. 'It was a revelation to be the patient and not the doctor in charge, and a blow to my pride to know that those gentle but devastating fingers held no feeling of intimacy for me, but were cool and practical, giving service but that's all.'

'Isn't that what good nursing's about?' Samantha was flushed and hoped the hat hid her expression. 'Whatever the nurse feels, whether it's indifference, dislike or even love, she must treat each patient in the same way, with equal care.'

'So I see. For you, no one person is special?' His eyes darkened and his mouth showed creases of bitterness.

'No patient must appear to be special, and yet each individual *is* special,' she said softly. 'But I have other facets to my nature, and my own private feelings.'

'Those that I shall never dare to explore, as you've made it clear that I'm your patient,' he stated, turning the car in an extravagant circle before parking in front of the hospital to a vacant space where it was clearly marked 'AMBULANCES'.

'And you have your own private life and loves in which I have no part,' she murmured, as he called to a porter to tell him where to find the ward in which Nathan was a patient.

'You go in. The porter says I can't park here, so

I'll meet you in the ward. What a come-down, to be in a place where I'm not known and respected, and everyone thinks of me as just another patient or a tiresome hospital visitor!'

Samantha glanced at the tight-fitting jeans that showed every line of his masculinity and the bright red and blue T-shirt open at the neck. 'You should have brought a white coat,' she said, and walked slowly into the cool foyer.

Dimly, she heard the urgency of the hospital emerging as she ventured further into the building. Voluble men talked in very loud voices by an elevator and a group of pretty nurses came towards her, dressed in slim white uniform dresses, and tiny caps that were only ornaments on piles of luxuriant dark hair. The pastel walls and tiled floors were cool after the bright sunlight, the bright colours and wonderful designs of the tiles making her pause to examine them more closely. Gleaming trolleys and equipment glimpsed in the ante-rooms of the wards showed her that this was a lively unit, efficient, spotless and the kind of hospital where any nurse could be happy.

She paused to look out of a window at the view of distant Vesuvius, and her interest quickened. After the carnival, she would dismiss '*il dottore*' from her mind, if not from her heart, and do all the things she had planned before she met him.

'You haven't got very far.' She turned as she heard the hurrying footsteps. 'You forgot the grapes,' Laurie said, and looked out of the window at the view she had been observing.

'It looks menacing from this angle,' she said. 'Is

that a cloud or a minor eruption at the top of the mountain?'

'Cloud, but there have been spurts of lava and hot steam from a few rifts in the sides. None this year,' he told her, 'but put on your running shoes if you see it happening.'

'It couldn't happen again, could it?'

'You mean the major eruption that killed Pompeii with stifling dust and ash, and Herculaneum with molten mud?' He shook his head. 'Unlikely, but they watch it all the time. Scientists with measuring instruments test the pressure each day, and they'd be able to give adequate warning, or so they tell us.' He looked up at the peak with sombre eyes. 'Who knows? Molten lava and erupting gases might have other ideas. Who can control the forces of nature, or of love?' In the empty corridor, he bent to kiss her lips almost sadly as she drew away, then he grinned. 'Just therapy, Nurse,' he said, then took her by the hand and strode along the corridor, with Samantha trying to keep up with him.

'You look OK,' Laurie said bracingly when Nathan sank back on the pillows and tried to look pathetic as soon as he saw Samantha.

'I'm bushed,' Nathan assured her, ignoring the doctor, who was now examining the chart and case sheet that were hanging by the X-ray viewer. 'The police gave me a tough time, but I blamed the accident on the state of the road at that bend and said it was impossible to see that the road twisted just there. Lucky for me that they had an accident there last week, and they obviously felt this was a black spot and the crash wasn't really my fault.' He

Romance!
Sensation!
Medical Romance!

Now available together in an exciting NEW six book selection...

Try one from each series on us... together with our cuddly Teddy and an extra Mystery Gift absolutely FREE!

Warm to the sheer joy and reap the rewards of true **Romance**. Follow every intriguing twist as romance turns to **Sensation.** And feel your temperature rise amidst the hectic world of **Medical Romance**.

Each contemporary story is packed with excitement, but above all - romance.

And to introduce this offer to you, we'll send you 1 Romance, 1 Sensation and 1 Medical Romance title, a cuddly Teddy plus a Mystery Gift, absolutely FREE when you complete and return this card. At the same time we'll reserve a subscription for you which means you could go on to enjoy:

- **Six brand NEW titles -**
  two titles from our Romance, Sensation and Medical Romance series sent direct to you every month.

- **Free Postage and Packaging -**
  we pay all the extras.

- **Free Monthly Newsletter -**
  packed with competitions, author news, horoscopes and much more.

- **Special Offers -**
  selected exclusively for our readers.

Claim your FREE books and gifts here

Yes Please send me three books and two gifts absolutely FREE. Please also reserve a special Reader Service subscription for me. If I decide to subscribe, I will receive two each of the very latest titles from the Mills & Boon Romance, Medical Romance and Silhouette Sensation series every month. Six books for just £10.10 postage and packing FREE, thats less than £1.70 per book. If I decide not to subscribe I shall write to you within 10 days. The FREE books and gifts remain mine to keep in any case. I understand that I am under no obligation whatsoever. I may cancel or suspend my subscription at any time simply by writing to you. I am over 18 years of age.

8A2X

Ms/Mrs/Miss/Mr _____

Address _____

_____

_____ Postcode _____

Signature _____

laughed. 'No breathalyser, as I was flat out of this world, and they couldn't even take a blood sample until I'd been treated here.'

'You're a very lucky man,' Laurie assured him. 'Gaol here isn't a good idea!'

Nathan shrugged. 'I had the feeling that the two policemen who came here weren't all that keen on paperwork and wanted out as soon as possible. One of them hardly listened to a thing I said as the nurse who was taking my blood-pressure had very nice boobs and a pair of very pretty legs. My secret weapon against the law! I owe her for that.' He took the grapes and chocolate and put them aside. 'I'll give her the chocolates.'

'Do you recall what happened?' asked Laurie.

'I told them I didn't remember a thing, but I do recall going over the side and a girl screaming.' He wrinkled his brow. 'Was there a girl? I don't remember having a passenger.'

'You're in for a bad time, Nathan,' Laurie said with satisfaction. 'Remember Rhoda from the language college?'

'Blonde, with the look of a junior table tennis champion? All fresh skin and wobbly boobs?'

Laurie chuckled. 'Boy, oh, boy, you are in trouble!' He winked at Samantha, who was giggling. 'I don't actually know if you proposed to her; you certainly filled her up with wine and flattery, told her she was the only girl you'd ever loved, and you dragged her screaming to the car to carry her off who knows where!'

'Oh, *no*! Is she OK?'

'A bit weepy after the accident, but fine now physically.'

'Only physically?' Nathan looked alarmed.

'She wanted to come to see you, but we advised her to let you rest,' Samantha said solemnly. 'But as soon as you're better, Nathan, she'll be there, all dewy-eyed, waiting for her lover.'

'Oh, no! I didn't *do* anything to her?'

'I think Samantha means the old meaning of lover. One who loves, not necessarily a sex fiend,' Laurie said. He glanced at Samantha with irony. 'There are many who love but get no further than first base.'

'And many who look and sound sincere but are really only passing the time.'

Laurie regarded her sharply, but she was looking at Nathan as if her remarks were meant for him alone.

'I wanted to date you, Sam,' Nathan said in an aggrieved voice. 'If you'd taken me in hand, this might never have happened.'

'Never call me that again,' she said firmly. 'Only one person called me Sam, and I didn't like it even then.' She realised that Laurie was watching her. 'Silly, I know, but I just don't like it,' she went on lamely, wishing she'd never mentioned the subject and had let Nathan, in his ignorance, continue to annoy her and bring back painful memories of the boy she had loved and who had drowned when canoeing on the River Wye.

What did it matter now? It was years ago, and she had been just a fresh-faced, slightly breathless teenager, a bit like Rhoda as far as her eagerness for adventure went, but being called Sam brought it all back; the week in Wales with the youth group and the wonder of riding white water in a flimsy canoe, evenings drinking Coke and eating the tough and filling pizzas supplied by the local youth hostel, and Julian, the boy with long fair hair and the awkward tenderness of youth, who said she was the best female canoeist he had ever met and kissed her with fervour and a complete lack of expertise.

'What happened to him?' Laurie asked quietly.

She shrugged. 'It was a long time ago.'

Nathan was selecting a grape with care. 'You've never forgotten him,' Laurie persisted.

'One never forgets the dead if they were loved,' she said simply. A nurse came to give Nathan his lunch and the visitors left.

'I'm sorry,' Laurie said when once again they were out in the hot sunshine.

'Sorry for what?' she asked.

'Sorry to think of you wasting your life and love on someone who died, as you said, long ago.' He tried to take her hand, but she froze. 'Life goes on, and we have to adapt to the future,' he went on. 'You can't carry a torch all your life for a man who's dead. You must learn to love again.'

'A lot of people think they can never give up the love of their lives,' she said quietly. 'I agree that it's a mistake to lose a chance of a new happiness, but you know that the past is a powerful enemy to new love.' She wanted to shake him and make him look at her with fresh awareness. Caterina's married, you fool! she thought. Can't you see any further than the end of your nose? You talk of it being wrong to hold on to the past, but you do just that with bitterness and great tenacity, and yet you want me. At times you really do want me.

'Let's go back,' he said, as if he wanted to end the conversation. 'I have phone calls to make, and I want to be there in case Sir Ralph needs picking up from the airport.'

'Ring the house now and ask Maria if he's been in touch. It would save you a long drive later if you knew he was expected soon.' Samantha sounded cool and businesslike and gave no hint of her inner turmoil.

'Good idea. If his plane is due within the next hour or so, what will you do? Come with me or stay in Naples for shopping and take a taxi back to the villa?'

'I might go back to Nathan and spend the afternoon there,' she said, and smiled.

'No!' He reddened. 'His scan is clear, but he ought to sleep a lot and be ready to come out of hospital all the quicker.' He relaxed. 'I can't wait to see his reunion with Rhoda.'

'There's a phone over there and it's fairly quiet now. I'll wait here until you get through and then decide what to do.'

She watched an ambulance arrive, followed by a car that screamed to a halt and disgorged a family of mother, sister or wife and two men, the women weeping and the men talking in loud voices as the patient was taken from the back of the ambulance. He appeared less upset than the family, and gave Samantha a fleeting embarrassed smile as if he didn't know what the fuss was about, before being taken into the building, followed by his family, who had no intention of missing any drama that might come from a fairly routine admission for a broken leg.

'Maria said Sir Ralph will be arriving in half an hour. His office faxed a message as soon as the plane left the UK.' Laurie found his car keys and looked at his watch. 'She was pleased to hear from me, as he likes to be met, and the gardener who acts as chauffeur when Sir Ralph is at the villa isn't available today. If he's on time and we allow half an hour for the airport formalities, we can just make it.'

Samantha hung back, unwilling to be rushed and regretting the loss of a shopping trip to the main streets of Naples. 'You go,' she said. 'I'll find my own way home.'

'I need you. I may have to stay with the car, or at least to look for a parking space while you stay by the barrier to collect him.'

The traffic was heavy, and Laurie said little before they reached the airport, apart from swearing gently under his breath at the crazy drivers of dented vehicles who thought they could creep into a space only wide enough to take a motorcycle. The many stops at lights and blocks of traffic congestion made Samantha anxious, but they arrived at the airport with about fifteen minutes to spare and she went to the barrier where others waited for relatives, and couriers from travel companies held up coloured umbrellas to gather their flocks about them when the package tour passengers disembarked.

Businessmen who had travelled light with only briefcases and hand luggage came through quickly as they had no need to wait for the luggage carousel to bring heavy bags from the plane. A trickle of

others followed, then Laurie arrived and could see
over the heads of most of the incoming passengers.
He waved and called, and Samantha recognised Sir
Ralph Gower, one of the world's leading surgeons,
but who now looked vaguely lost amid the din and
hassle of the airport.

With obvious relief he saw Laurie and pushed his
luggage trolley towards him. 'Hello, my dear boy,'
he said. 'I can't say how very glad I am to see you. I
hate this part of any journey.'

'Stay with Samantha while I fetch the car and
bring it to the exit over there,' Laurie said.

'You look much better.' Sir Ralph regarded
Samantha with affection. 'Maria feeding you up, is
she? Good. I want you back on duty ready to scrub
for me, but not before you're really well.' They
walked towards the exit, pushing the heavy trolley.
'Now tell me how my naughty children are behav-
ing.' He gave a dry chuckle. 'I've had one card from
Sarah and no visits from the police, so I assume
they're still alive and haven't burned the villa down.
Any unsuitable entanglements?' he asked with a
touch of real anxiety.

'No. They have a fairly normal circle of friends,
and Mark is busy sick-visiting a girl from the
language school who had toxic shock syndrome but
is making a very good recovery. He seems very
interested in her, but I think you'll find he has a
more mature outlook than he did at home, and
Sarah seems to know the difference between good
and bad eggs.'

She told him about the accident and reassured him
that the villa was not involved and that the police

seemed satisfied that it was the fault of the bad road and the absence of street lighting and warning signs that had contributed most to the car going over into the terrace.

'A lucky escape,' he agreed. 'One that need not interfere with the carnival.' He smiled. 'In England, I shy away from anything like that, but here it's a pure medieval tapestry rolled out once every four years and full of wonderful sounds and colour. I've been to it three times, and each time I find it most satisfying.'

'I've been persuaded to wear a very beautiful dress that must be very old and valuable,' Samantha said. 'Do you think anyone will take offence if I do wear it, as I'm not a local woman and have no roots in Italy?'

'You'll be with Laurie?' He nodded as if that made everything right. 'I recall the last time, four years ago, when Laurie took part, looking very fine and handsome in his costume. On that occasion he led Caterina to the revels. She looked exquisite, and I think she met the man she's now married at those celebrations.' He sighed. 'Sometimes Laurie can be a bit pigheaded. He was dead against the marriage, but I think she was right. A slightly neurotic woman doesn't need a doctor for a husband, however devoted he might be. She needs sheltering and a marriage to a man with lots of money to give her everything she thinks she needs, not the life of a busy doctor's wife, hearing about other people's diseases and imagining she has them too.'

'She's very beautiful,' Samantha remarked. 'I saw the wedding the day after I came to Amalfi.'

'Lovely as a flower,' he agreed. 'But bright flowers fade in the sun, my dear. An English rose blooms for far longer.' He laughed. 'Don't look like that. Has someone made this particular rose unhappy?'

'That's Laurie's car,' she said, and hurried with the trolley to help pack the baggage into the trunk.

'Let's get out of here,' said Sir Ralph. 'I hope Maria has something light for my lunch. I refused the plastic tray on the plane, which will please her. I had a glass of champagne and a savoury, but I shall swear that nothing passed my lips on the flight. That will make sure I have her complete devotion all the time I'm here, even if I work in the clinic at night and put meals out of schedule.'

'I alerted the clinic and they have a few cases lined up for tomorrow,' said Laurie. 'There's one man you saw in London who's ready for operation here as his family live in Sorrento and want to be near him, and two patients who were referred to you for second opinions by your old friend Professor Karl Balsar from Geneva. Possible surgery in both cases.' Laurie paused as if choosing his words carefully. 'I spoke to the professor on the phone and asked if he'd seen Caterina.'

'It's early yet,' Sir Ralph said, and frowned. 'She's agreed to follow her husband's wishes first. He's well meaning and cares for her and I'm sure will never let her be in real danger. You worry about her far too much,' he added firmly. 'She's married now and even her close family have no direct responsibility for her. We're just old friends, Laurie. Dear friends, but distanced by her marriage. I must visit her parents—I enjoy their local wine and they make good pasta. Maybe they've heard something that we don't know.'

Samantha stared ahead as she sat in the back seat of the car, unable to avoid hearing everything they said. Laurie was an example of everything good in a man. He was handsome and intelligent and strong and very virile. He had skills that many men would envy and enough charisma to charm a woman so that she wanted to surrender completely to his body and his desires, and yet in this one way he was weak. He loved a woman so completely that he couldn't accept the fact that he no longer had a part in her life. Even now when she was on her honeymoon he was thinking of her far more than was healthy. A honeymoon was a private and precious time for newly-weds in love.

Sarah ran to meet her father with every sign of pleasure, and Mark followed, more slowly, but wearing a big smile. A happy family, Samantha decided with a tinge of envy. Sarah tucked her hand under her father's arm and took him indoors to a rapturous welcome from Maria, who was convinced that only her good cannelloni would restore him after his terrible journey through the air with nothing to eat.

Samantha walked to her room alone to freshen up. Of Laurie there was no sign, as he had gone as soon as he parked the car under a shady tree as if he might require it later. He didn't join them for lunch.

CHAPTER SIX

'WE'LL have to make a very early start,' Laurie said. He looked tired, as Sir Ralph had operated on three cases in the clinic that afternoon and one of them had given them cause for concern, which meant that Laurie had gone back to check on the care the man was receiving and found that he had to stay until late, trying to find a collapsed vein that the more junior doctor couldn't locate. While recovering from the anaesthetic, the patient had dragged out the first drip and he needed fluids urgently, but it was difficult setting up a fresh one, even with a thin cannula.

Maria looked as anxious as a mother hen and hovered over him with another helping of lasagne. 'You must eat or you will be sick,' she warned sternly. 'Tomorrow you must be strong and handsome, so eat and go to sleep.'

'At least I've handed him over to an efficient doctor now, and the patient's condition is improving,' Laurie said. 'Sir Ralph will go in tomorrow, but my part there is over.' He laughed. 'Maria, that's enough. I shall be too fat to wear my costume and too heavy to dance tomorrow night if you continue to force-feed me.'

Samantha sipped her fresh orange juice and wished she had been with him all day, but Sir Ralph had dismissed her firmly when she offered to help.

'You're here on holiday, and although you had a clear throat swab you should wait until you're really fit before you go into an operating theatre,' he said.

'I am clear. I had two clear swabs before I came away, and I feel fine,' she protested.

'Save your energies for the carnival and to making sure that Laurie enjoys it too. He works very hard at Beattie's and needs to back-pedal a little. The trouble with men like him is that they're so good that they get work thrust on them. It happened to me when I was a registrar, but now I pick and choose what I do, and I confess I leave a lot to men like him.'

Sir Ralph was probably sound asleep now, safe in the knowledge that Laurie had made sure the patient was fine, Samantha decided. She had been reading a book in the sitting-room when she heard the sound of Laurie's car on the gravel drive. She liked to think that she was not waiting to hear him come back to the villa, but as soon as he did arrive she closed her book and walked across the hall to the stairs, to go to her room, but Maria, who had obviously been watching for him, came out and asked her to carry a tray into the dining-room while she fetched bread.

Laurie sat down heavily. 'Thanks,' he said, with a tired smile. 'I'm ravenous.' Samantha turned to go, but he called her back. 'Stay and talk,' he begged. 'I need to clear my mind before I sleep, and we have to be up early.' Obediently she sat at the table, and Maria brought her some fresh orange juice to make sure she stayed for a while, and Samantha watched Laurie eat his belated dinner.

'Why so early?' she wanted to know. 'The procession doesn't start until the afternoon.'

'We'd never get near Amalfi if we leave it until then. A friend has an apartment overlooking the main road, and we're invited there to have lunch and then to change into the costumes.'

'What happens?' she asked. 'I know there are certain traditions, but I'm not sure what's expected of me.'

Laurie drained his wine glass and took one of the tiny almond biscuits that Maria had placed on a pretty plate on the table. 'That's better,' he said, and watched Samantha load the tray with the used crockery before taking it to the kitchen, where she insisted that *il dottore* was well fed and needed nothing more, so Maria could go to her well-earned rest.

'More coffee?' she asked.

He shook his head. 'I'm going to bed. Tomorrow we breakfast at eight and pack what we want to wear for the evening as we shall be away from here all day.'

'But Amalfi isn't that far away,' she said.

'It is when the traffic's bumper to bumper and some roads are shut to cars. This is *the* event of the year, and attracts a lot of visitors.'

'What do I have to do?' she asked again.

He took her by the shoulders, and she was aware of his nearness, his tired body and his need for a physical contact that was more friendly than sexual. 'You have nothing to do but smile and look beautiful. You'll walk to the cathedral from a big hotel on the main road, while the whole of Amalfi and lots of

gawping visitors exclaim at your beauty, then you'll
sit listening but not understanding a word while a
service is in progress in the cathedral, before joining
the procession again, down the red-carpeted steps
and along the road, up to the hotel by the Saracen
tower.'

'And then?'

'Guido will cover your hands with kisses and tell
you that you're the most lovely creature in Amalfi,
and that his ancestors would have been proud you
wore the dress.'

'Is that all?' she asked.

'No. Guido will expect me to kiss you and thank
you for your part in the procession—like this.'
Laurie bent his neck and his mouth on hers tasted of
almonds and tenderness. He smiled as she half
closed her eyes, and her body moved closer to his.
'Guido will expect this as he believes we're lovers,
and you wouldn't like to hurt him and his very nice
family, would you?'

'It's all a part of the revels,' Samantha agreed
demurely.

'Exactly.' He kissed her again, his lips mobile and
demanding, and she felt her heart flutter like an
imprisoned bird. 'That's good for a rehearsal,' he
said. 'Tomorrow we should be quite convincing.'

'You did say we have to be ready by eight
tomorrow morning,' she reminded him, and pushed
him gently away, but her eyes held a soft expression.
He might be in love with another woman, but his
mouth was all a girl needed to fill the emptiness of
her heart, and if he was only play-acting, there was
no harm, was there?

She closed the front door after him as he went back to the cottage and she walked slowly to her room, feeling warm and somehow radiant, with a glow that she knew was not hers by right, and dreamed of scarlet cloaks and high banners and a face that was as handsome as those on any medieval tapestry.

Samantha stretched and turned off her alarm clock, and heard movements in the rooms below her bedroom. A thrill of excitement when she realised that today was the day of the procession made her leap out of bed and hurry through her shower and make-up, using only light moisturiser and a dash of rosy lipstick.

She packed the ancient gown carefully in its box and pulled a soft-top suitcase from her wardrobe. She stopped to think what she'd need, and laughed softly as she knew she must pack almost as much for one day as she would need for a week: make-up and toilet things, fresh underwear and tights, and something to wear for the evening revels as the gown was far too precious to wear while dancing. She frowned. The skirt of thin cotton that she now wore was pretty, but more suitable for the beach or sightseeing than for a more formal setting. The sleeveless camisole of lilac and the floral pattern on the skirt needed bare legs and espadrilles or linen loafers, not the pretty high-heeled sandals that she had in her luggage and would wear during the day.

I need a completely different outfit for this evening, she decided, and took out the new dress she had bought in Positano. If I'm to lose myself in pure

Italiana today, I might as well wear it, and it will give me courage to put it on when we get back to England and I go to a more ordinary dance. The soft fabric sighed through her hands as she folded it and put it with the other clothes, and a pair of sandals with single golden toe-thongs might do if she needed lower heels later.

'Ready?' asked Laurie as she sat down to breakfast. He was bright and looked as if he had never done anything more strenuous yesterday than get up and have a shower and lie by the pool all day.

'I think so, but as soon as we reach Amalfi I know I shall remember something I need.' Samantha regarded him with concern. 'What about the dressing? Have we time to do that before we leave?'

'No, I asked the sister in the clinic to do that when I was stripped off for scrubbing for the case, and it doesn't need anything more than a dusting of sulphonamide powder and a dry dressing, so we can leave it for a day or so. She'll see to it when I visit the clinic again.'

'Fine.' Samantha tried to smile and wondered why she felt badly about being relieved of her duty. 'Did she get rid of the rest of the spots?' she asked.

'Yes, she was a bit more forceful than you, and I felt as if I'd been scrubbed with a wire brush! Don't look so pleased. I didn't enjoy it. Her hands weren't at all like yours.'

'Bracing friction is good for the skin, I believe. Why not buy a loofah and do it all yourself in future now that the skin is intact?'

'If she attacks me again I shall run screaming to you for gentle massage,' he threatened, and got up from the table with a meaningful glint in his dark blue eyes. 'Who knows what might happen this time?'

'Hair-grips! If I'm to wear that gauzy veil thing on my head I'll need to anchor it firmly,' Samantha said hastily, and escaped to her room until she heard the car horn warning her that she must be ready to leave.

To her intense relief, their hostess was a British air stewardess, married to an Italian, who spoke perfect English, and Samantha and Carol took to each other at once. The gown was taken out and spread on the bed and admired, and the new dress was put on a hanger on the side of the wardrobe.

'Are you going to be in the procession?' Samantha asked.

'No. It's sheer luck that I'm here at all. I thought I was on the Singapore run, but the flight was cancelled through engine trouble. I did have some leave due, so here I am.' Carol sighed. 'A whole week with Luciano. It's bliss!' She looked crisp and cool, with a flawless complexion and expert eye make-up, and Samantha could imagine her looking great in uniform. 'Have you known Laurie long?' she asked when he was unpacking his gear in another room.

'Not before this holiday.'

Carol raised her eyebrows. 'I thought you were very good friends.' The implication was there that she meant that Laurie and Samantha were lovers. 'Guido seems to think we shall see you posing on the steps of Amalfi cathedral soon, in billowy white.'

'No!' Samantha laughed uneasily. 'We met

through Sir Ralph Gower.' She explained how she had come to be in Italy, and Carol nodded but looked disappointed. 'I'm really on sick leave from the hospital where I am in training in London,' she said.

'Damn! I thought you'd marry Lorenzo and live here where we could be friends. It's good to speak my own language and not have to struggle for words.'

'Laurie isn't here very often,' Samantha reminded her. 'He works at Beattie's in London too, and there he's Laurie Martin, a very English doctor, so I'm told.' She smiled at Carol's disappointed expression. 'You aren't here very often either, except between flights, and only then if you happen to end the run in Italy. We might meet in London when you have time off there. That could be fun.'

'Give me your address and where I can reach you by phone. Here's my card with a business number in London and the one here.' Carol eyed Samantha with speculation. 'Sure that you and Lorenzo aren't——?'

'Quite sure. Someone I loved died, and Laurie is still in love with someone who married another man, so we're really just friendly professional contacts and that's all.'

Poor sweet Julian, she thought with a twinge of conscience. I haven't thought of you for a long time except with sad affection. Even my guilty feelings have faded, as I know that the fact that we had a tiff the night before you died had nothing to do with the accident.

'A patient?' queried Carol. 'Was he a patient?'

'No, he died canoeing in Wales, and it was a long time ago,' Samantha added, to make up for any deception.

'I didn't know about Laurie. Luciano has said nothing. I can't believe it. Luciano would know, and he'd tell me. Men gossip even more than women, especially the Italians! Talking of weddings, did you see Caterina when she was married? I wanted to be here, but I was in Fiji that day and missed it. I can't wait to see the photographs.'

'You know her?' Samantha felt her face stiffen, but she managed to smile. 'She looked breathtaking. I was in Amalfi town just by chance and saw her on the cathedral steps. Then I met Laurie, who was watching her too, and we found that we were going to the same villa.'

It sounded smooth enough, and Carol couldn't know how that chance meeting had coloured everything Samantha did and thought since that moment.

'She's like a china doll,' Carol said. 'Fragile but able to get what she wants, and she wanted Paolo and all that he can give her, even if he is a bit of a crank when it comes to health matters.' She laughed. 'Sir Ralph and Lorenzo disapprove, I know, as she has had a niggling pain for ages and a lot of time in bed over the past six months, but Paolo swears that his friend in Geneva can cure everything with tinctures and homoeopathic medicines.'

'Why is he so sure?' asked Samantha.

'The doctor's very skilled and has a lot of successes to his name. He cured Paolo's sister of asthma and his mother of a skin complaint, so Paolo goes to him for any treatment he thinks necessary, believing he can work miracles. Being as healthy as an ox himself, he hasn't had to put the choice between surgery and fringe medicine to the test before now.'

She shrugged. 'Lorenzo may be right to want her to see a surgeon, but I'm inclined to agree with Caterina. Anything's better than the knife, so she went into this willingly, and they're in the clinic in Geneva now.'

'What if this doesn't work?' queried Samantha.

'Then she'll see a surgeon.'

'Someone like Sir Ralph or Laurie?' Samantha licked her dry lips.

'Sir Ralph would do it if she has it done here among her friends and relatives, but not Lorenzo. He was always too close to the family and he might feel too involved.'

'That makes sense.' Samantha looked at Carol and wondered how she couldn't see just how it did make sense. Laurie was far too much in love with the girl ever to want to touch her with a scalpel.

Carol shuddered slightly. 'If I had to have surgery I'd want to go away where nobody knew me, and then I could shout and scream to my heart's content without trying to be brave for the sake of appearances. Imagine knowing the doctor who stood over you, wearing a mask and gloves! Even worse if you liked him or were in love with him!'

'Worse still for the surgeon if he was in love with the patient,' Samantha said softly.

'Coffee,' called Luciano.

'Orange juice for me, darling,' Carol replied. 'Don't drink it if it's too strong, Samantha. Luciano makes coffee like tar and adds half a cup of sugar!

Delicious, but I can't take it more than once a day or my skin would soon show signs of wear! I'll boil some water and you can dilute it. Whenever we go out, I order more water in a separate jug if we have coffee. The Italians think I'm mad, but visitors see what I'm doing and quickly learn the right phrase to ask for more hot water, then they can use it and get diluted coffee while they're in Italy.'

Lunch was a simple salad with chicken and fresh fruit, then Carol helped Samantha to dress. The gown fell gracefully to her ankles and the gleam of silk and velvet made the whole garment rich in texture. 'Thank heavens for nurses' white-headed cap pins and a few hair-grips,' Samantha said as she secured the wisp of gauzy silk veil to her hair.

'Just a touch of blusher and a hint of powder,' Carol suggested, and outlined Samantha's eyes with light, swift strokes of the pencil. 'There, straight from a Renaissance painting, but I believe we can't have any idea about the magnificence of the rest of the procession until we see it all. I came here first two years ago, and there hasn't been one during that time.'

A trumpet sounded and a piccolo traced a scale over the beat of a drum, somewhere up the hill, and Carol leaned out of the window of the sitting-room. 'Luciano is waving. We ought to go down,' she said, then laughed. 'If you want Lorenzo for more than work, you'd better get busy. He looks superb! Oh, dear, I can see at least two women eyeing him with acute hunger. Forget all your old loves and marry this marvellous man. If I weren't hooked on my husband I'd make a play for him myself.'

'Where is he?' Samantha peered down at the now busy street. Cars lined the verges, but the free run of traffic had been stopped and men and women in costume milled about, chattering and laughing, making the grey road alive with scarlet and purple and green against a vivid blue sky.

She caught her breath. Laurie stood across the road, taller than most of the men, his slim hips and long legs encased closely in scarlet tights under a sumptuous robe that reached his thighs, but was slit at the sides, so that as he walked the lines of his body could be seen. His shoulders were broad under rich gold thread and scarlet and gold velvet, and on his head he wore a rakish cap of scarlet silk and miniver.

Samantha gulped, and Carol laughed. 'Be careful if you don't want to fall in love today. I think I'll wear dark glasses. Husbands are jealous here, and I might find my gaze wandering a bit, even if I am devoted to Luciano.'

'What if he has the same idea?' queried Samantha.

Carol looked complacent. 'He'll look, but he'd never touch. I shall wear a very short pale yellow shift, and only gold ear-rings as jewellery. The cool, untouched look gets him really turned on, and if I can't wear anything as glamorous as you have I want to be different.'

The bright sunlight made the dress glisten like a mother-of-pearl shell, and Laurie stopped talking when he saw the two girls emerge from the doorway, one slight and long-legged in the absurdly brief mini of palest yellow, making a foil for the dress that had seen so many of these festivals over the years, and just as a jewel was best seen against a plain background, so did Samantha's gown glow as if on honey silk.

He walked towards them slowly, his mouth stern as if he was trying to control a deep emotion, but his enigmatic gaze gave no hint if that emotion was anger, disapproval or a great sensuality.

'Here she is, your paramour for the day, Lorenzo,' Carol said with a throaty chuckle. She gave Samantha a wicked look. 'There's Luciano with some competition. I'd better get to him before the harpies tear him to shreds. See you later.'

'Come over here and look at the sea,' Laurie said. He took Samantha by the hand. 'You look beautiful,' he whispered.

'You're pretty, too, sir,' she replied lightly, but her heart beat faster and the touch of their hands made her want to lure him on to more extravagant pledges of love.

'Look down there.' She stood on tiptoe and saw the wide bay of Naples and the Amalfian coast dotted with small craft. Two long boats, each with a high prow and eight bronzed oarsmen, were being urged on in a race. The man on each stern waved and shouted, and their gold and green suits added to the spectacle as the gilded flying horses of the delicate figureheads cleft the blue water, dividing the waves and leaving a flurry of white water behind the boats.

'It's magic,' breathed Samantha. She felt Laurie's lips on her hair and on her cheek and heard endearments in Italian. Gone was the serious English doctor. Here was a knight of long ago, passionate and proud in the memory of ancient rites, secure in his arrogance and sure of his place of importance in society.

A man called and he turned slightly to listen, then laughed and pointed down towards the boats. 'Guido's on the far stern,' he said. 'Today he's a very important man who urges his men to victory, and later he'll be one of the honoured few who bear the silver statue of St Andrew, the patron saint of fishermen, up the steps to the cathedral.'

'Why do they do that?' she asked.

'Tradition, to take the Saint to be blessed and to ask him to bless the boats and the fish for the coming year.' Laurie smiled and was once again more English, with laughing eyes. 'I tell him he'll have a hernia if he does it for another festival. He's put a lot of weight on since the last one. The statue's two and a half metres tall, and there are a lot of steps up to the cathedral!'

'And I'm wearing this?' Samantha touched the dress with reverent fingers. 'I had no idea how important today would be to him and to his family.'

'Talking of Guido's family, come and meet them at the hotel up there. We have time before we're called by a blast of trumpets to take our places.'

Samantha was too fascinated to feel embarrassed. Four women almost drowned her in compliments and tears, and she learned that she was like a girl who had worn the dress in the past, and nobody in memory had worn it with more dignity, more beauty, more grace, more. . .everything. She also caught a reference to marriage and looked puzzled, but was made to stand by the flower-covered wall and have her photograph taken several times, to compare with the picture of that other girl who had a place of honour in Guido's house.

'Did you understand all that?' Laurie asked as he led her away when the first blast of music summoned them to assemble. He sounded cautious, and looked relieved when she said she had missed three-quarters of what was said but had caught the drift of it.

'I gather they like the way I look!' she said, laughing, 'but I didn't hear who's getting married.'

He reddened, then said hastily, 'They referred to the marriage of the sea with the great cities of the past—Venice, Pisa and Genoa, and the triumph over the pirates who were the scourge of this coast long ago.' He looked innocent, but she didn't believe a word. The women were too busy shedding sentimental tears to be talking of pirates and Venice!

The afternoon and evening passed in a whirl of movement, colour and music, and Samantha was lost in admiration of the people who organised and took part in the revels. The pageant ended at last, the trumpeters put away their brass and silver instruments and the streets cleared. Samantha and Laurie went back to the apartment, where Guido caught up with them.

Carefully, after more compliments and thanks from Guido, who seemed to have a stiff shoulder after his efforts with the statue, Samantha took off the dress and packed it carefully in its box ready for Guido to take away. He was drinking red wine and boasting of his team's win in the regatta, and he stared as she came into the room carrying the box and now changed into the Italian dress she had bought in Positano.

'Ah, *bellissima*!' he exclaimed. 'You are a very lucky man, Lorenzo.' He winked. 'Do not make babies until after the next festival,' he said and laughed. 'The dress will not fit after that. Wine makes my suit tight and nearly strangles me, and love makes women comfortable and fat.'

'I shan't be here for the next festival,' Samantha began, then saw his surprised expression. 'That is, who knows where we all shall be?' she added piously.

'You will come!' he said. 'You will wear that dress once again and be one of us.'

'I'll do my best to keep her slim,' Laurie said smoothly, and Guido smiled again. Samantha shrugged and sipped some white wine and water. Next year, or at least in four years' time, everyone here would have forgotten that she had ever existed, and plans would be made for another girl with a good figure and bright smile to wear the dress and be a princess for a day.

Carol came into the sitting-room with a big smile on her face. She was dressed in a blue mini-dress with glass beads trimming the edge of the low neckline and bringing a trail of perfume and fresh shampoo. 'How much of the festival did you see?' asked Guido with a grin.

'Quite a lot,' Carol said. 'We watched the parade and then Luciano felt too tired to go to church, so we took a long siesta, didn't we, darling?' she said as her husband came into the room, his hair still damp from the shower.

'And now I am very tired,' he said with satisfaction. 'And my wife tells me that I have to dance all night.' He laughed. 'She is cunning. She loves to dance and I shall have no more energy left for love now, so we dance while other men burn.' He glanced at Laurie with wickedly smiling eyes. 'Is that not so, my friend?'

'You may be right,' Laurie agreed, without expression as if the subject bored him. 'I'm hungry, and I have to get out of this gear. Excuse me while I change.'

'We're all going to the same party, I believe,' Carol said. 'Caterina's parents have invited a lot of people who couldn't be at the wedding and they asked us to come too. I was away, and Luciano was working.'

'Laurie was at the wedding,' Samantha told her.

'Of course.' Luciano looked surprised. 'But Laurie is invited to everything, as he has always been close to them.'

'Ready? I think we can get away now if we avoid the square by the cathedral. The traffic has almost gone as people go in search of food, and Isabella will expect us.' Laurie turned to Samantha. 'Bring your case, as we shall not come back here.' He fetched the car, and Guido disappeared to fetch his own car for his wife and daughters. The cases were put in the trunk and Samantha glanced at the man by her side in the car. He was dressed in a pure white suit with a pale blue shirt and dark tie, and looked as if he had never set foot in England.

What am I doing here? she wondered. I'd never met any of these colourful and warm people two

weeks ago, and yet now I'm with them, a part of
them, and I'm even dressed like an Italian girl! A
sudden vision of London on a grey day made her
smile wistfully. It was another world, and one she
could well put off seeing for a very long time.

'That was a sad sigh,' Laurie said softly, as he
drove slowly through the town. 'Tired or bored?'

'Neither. Just thinking that I have to leave this
place soon and I'll miss it all.'

'You won't miss it for long. As soon as you get
back you'll be caught up in another world, the world
you know and love,' he replied. 'I do the same, and
even Carol couldn't live here for keeps. She gets
tired of the eternal blue of the sea, believe it or not,
and now that Luciano has travelled a lot on business
he's used to being in different countries and enjoys
change as much as Carol does.'

'Where will they settle eventually?' she asked, but
she didn't ask the couple in the back seat as they
were too busy in deep conversation to hear her.

'They're buying an apartment in London soon and
will have the ideal answer to the situation. I'd like
that too,' he added. 'What do you think?'

'I could never afford two flats,' Samantha said
with regret. 'I love it here, but if I'm to see the
world I must be free to wander during my holidays,
or I shall see very little of all the wonderful places of
which I've read.' She leaned back in the seat so that
he couldn't read her face. If he was not there, would
the sun be as bright or the sea as blue, and would
she want to be there without him?

'Here we are.' He drove round to the back of a
huge house and they walked to the front door. Fairy

lights glittered over the terrace and in the trees, and
music came softly over the lawn.

Dancing had begun, and Samantha melted into
the arms of the man she loved, as soon as the music
changed and he drew her close to dance to an old
and sentimental tune. She closed her eyes and they
danced in silence, his body hard against her soft
thighs and his lips touching her hair. It was heaven,
and yet she was sad. Was he thinking of another,
completely unobtainable girl, trying to imagine that
she was in his arms instead of a substitute?

The music stopped, and they wandered to the
buffet where a group of highly excited people talked
of the day's happenings and ate the salads and
cooked meats, and the delicately flavoured sorbets.
They drank cool white wine and heady reds from
priceless Venetian glasses, and Laurie smiled tend-
erly as if Samantha was the only girl in the world for
him.

Perhaps a miracle has happened, she thought.
Perhaps he does love me and has put Caterina from
his heart for ever. She was aware of his need for her
love, the desire that had blossomed as they danced,
and she remembered Carol's expression when she
had appeared after a long and passionate siesta with
her husband. Samantha could think of no other word
for it but bliss.

Carol regarded her with malicious interest. 'I
thought you were still in mourning for a lost love,'
she said, nibbling a chicken drumstick. 'Sex makes
me hungry. I shall get as fat as that woman over
there.'

'Not you,' Samantha said with conviction.

'What gives with you and Lorenzo? I asked Luciano and he knows of no woman who broke Lorenzo's heart. It's no use, you can't keep anything to yourself here. They like to know *everything*, and I'm getting to be as bad.'

'He convinced me,' Samantha said, her earlier happiness fading as she recalled Laurie's pale face as he watched Caterina come down the cathedral steps and knew that she really was married and he had no part in her future. Together the two girls found the suite put aside for the ladies and repaired smudged lipstick after the food.

'I still think you're mistaken,' said Carol. 'Luciano says Lorenzo is mad about you.'

'Lorenzo may be, as a part of the revels and just because I'm here and I'm a woman. The costumes, the music and the romantic atmosphere make it impossible not to feel some attraction. He's only human. I felt it too,' Samantha admitted, 'but back at Beattie's I think Dr Laurie Martin will be far more reserved and formal and will forget I ever existed.'

'Rubbish,' Carol said with less certainty. 'Come on, you have to dance. Enjoy what you have, and don't cry for the moon,' she added. 'Life is short, but bits of it can be very sweet. Take my favourite saying to heart: "The now is good."' She laughed. 'If I die in a plane crash I shall have enjoyed my life. If I live to a ripe old age, I shall continue grabbing life with both hands and making it work for me. I'm right, you know. Take what offers and have no regrets even if it isn't permanent. Now back to the dance.'

CHAPTER SEVEN

'I FEEL like Cinderella,' Samantha said, not knowing whether to laugh or cry.

'I've made some hot chocolate. Let's drink it on the terrace. It's far too warm to sleep, but I like a comforting hot drink rather than a cold one when I can't sleep.' Sarah sounded older and almost maternal as she saw the unshed tears and the distraught hands plucking at the beautiful dress. 'Change into trousers, or the bugs on the terrace will get you. At least the dress didn't turn to rags when the ball was over,' she added with an attempt at humour.

'And it was nearly dawn and not midnight when my coach turned into a pumpkin,' Samantha said wryly.

'I suppose Laurie took the car?'

'Of course. He had to get to the clinic to pick up the ambulance and get to the airport fast, and Sir Ralph was busy making sure the clinic was ready to receive her.'

Sarah put a tin of biscuits on the tray and took it out to the terrace, while Samantha hurried to change into a high-necked yellow cotton sweater and jeans. She remembered the insect-repellent spray as she knew that all flying bugs adored Sarah's blood and would home in from miles away if her skin was exposed on the terrace.

The simple act of finding the spray and thinking

of something other than her own misery had a calming effect, and when she walked out into the warm, sweet-scented night she looked almost normal. She handed Sarah the spray and sat down at the wrought-iron table.

'I didn't light the lamp as it attracts all the moths,' Sarah said. 'There's enough moon and a hint of dawn, which will be enough.' She produced a battery-operated whisk and made the chocolate really frothy and creamy. 'I don't like it muddy,' she explained.

'It's delicious. I haven't tasted anything like it since a visit to Switzerland two years ago,' said Samantha.

'I made the biscuits too,' Sarah told her with pride. 'After a rocky start, Maria and I are really good together, and she's teaching me to cook. When I get back, I'm changing my course to catering. I'm glad I've been doing languages, as that will be useful when I'm a famous international chef.'

'I was surprised to find anyone about,' Samantha said. 'Did you go in to Amalfi?'

'Not this evening. I saw you in the parade and was madly jealous and hoped you'd be so fat the next time they have the revels that I'd be able to take your place.' Sarah laughed. 'They had a disco at the hostel until two in the morning, and we walked back from there. Mark and a couple more who crashed out on the living-room floor here as they were too bushed to go back again came back with me, but nobody was driving, after what happened to Nathan and Rhoda.'

'Maybe the shock of that had a good side after

all,' Samantha said. She stared into the grey horizon.
All shocks weren't as beneficial.

Sarah came over to refill her mug. 'And when I
came out here to have a think, what did I find?' She
clucked in imitation of Maria. '*Mamma mia*, I found
a weeping woman who looked so wild, I thought I
might have to dive into the pool and save her from
drowning!'

'You little liar!' Samantha laughed. 'I was a bit
tear-stained, I admit, and feeling miserable, but
suicide? Never!'

'What a pity—I've never saved anyone from
drowning. Think of the headlines, with huge pictures
of me looking modest and saying it was nothing,
really nothing at all. "Beautiful teenage English girl
risks her life for her friend." Then cameras flashing
everywhere I went in Amalfi, as I'm discovered by
the Press.'

'Thanks for the chocolate. I think I'll go to bed
for what's left of the night.' Samantha put her mug
on the tray.

'You owe me,' said Sarah. 'I promise I won't tell.
I can be as tight as an oyster when I have to be, but
I'm dying to know.'

'There's really nothing to tell. Cinderella went to
the ball, overstayed her time and came home in a
taxi alone.'

'Not even a tiny bit of mayhem or rape?' Sarah
looked very disappointed.

'We were dancing when a message came for
Laurie to get to a phone. He came back and said
he'd have to leave and had asked Luciano to get me
a taxi.'

Said like that, it sounded so ordinary, but Sarah would never know the feelings that had stabbed at her heart when Laurie came back from the telephone, grim-faced and suddenly formal.

When he went to the phone, he had left her with obvious reluctance, with a whispered aside: 'It will have to be something very important to get me away from you tonight, *cara.*' They had planned to go down at dawn to watch the fishing boats come in and have breakfast at a small *trattoria* that made delicious omelettes. He had kissed her cheek and called her *cara*, and she had waited with a smile on her lips, convinced that she had won his love. He desired her, she knew, and now, after this magical day, she thought he loved her, but then something really important to him had turned up, making him rush away to the side of the woman he really loved, leaving the girl who had made his day and evening pleasant and was good for a flirtation and more, but not real love.

'He came back here, before going to the clinic. Why couldn't he bring you back at the same time?' Sarah wanted to know. 'That's what made me think you'd had a terrible row.'

'I suppose he wanted to think out what to do next,' Samantha said, trying to be reasonable. 'I couldn't help. Sir Ralph made that quite clear earlier when I'd offered to help at the clinic, and when an emergency erupts there's no place for passengers to get in the way.' She sighed. 'I do know how it is. When I worked in Casualty we often had to keep relatives and friends away who were very concerned about a patient but who held up the work by standing too close and by just being there in the way, often offering help that was of no use and even trying to suggest methods of treatment!'

'But you're a nurse and have the experience they need. I'd have thought Laurie would have grabbed you to help.' Sarah sounded indignant. 'Spoiled bitch,' she said, with feeling. 'Who but Caterina would expect a private ambulance jet to pick her up in the middle of the night and expect another private ambulance to be waiting at the airport to take her to the clinic without even asking if it was all right for her to go there? What if all the rooms had been full?'

'We don't know the full story,' Samantha said quietly. 'If she's really ill, then of course she wanted to be with her family and friends, and if an operation is necessary, then Sir Ralph would be my first choice for anything to do with the abdomen and gynae complaints.'

'I bet she came dressed in a lovely nightie, with her make-up perfect, and insisted on having at least five huge suitcases packed for the visit.'

'If this was a sudden decision she wouldn't have had time for all that, and if she was feeling ill she couldn't have done a lot,' Samantha protested.

'She wouldn't, but she'd make sure that others did everything she wanted,' said Sarah. 'Other people's time, not her own, Samantha. You obviously haven't met Caterina. She's sweet and beautiful and can charm the birds from the trees, but she gets what she wants even if it hurts other people, and then looks all dewy-eyed and hurt and asks in a little-girl voice if she should have done whatever it was.

Everyone reassures her and believes she really didn't mean to be a nuisance, and she gives a smug little smile and goes on her own sweet way.' Sarah looked pensive. 'I can't help thinking she has everyone on the end of a very thick string and she isn't as ill as she makes out.'

'You don't like her!' said Samantha, surprised.

'Oh, I do. She can be fun, and besides, I'm studying her methods. I shall get my own way just as she does, by copying her,' Sarah said cheerfully.

'Maybe you should change your course to psychiatry.'

'That's a good idea. At least I made you laugh.'

'I was amused at the thought of you going all dewy-eyed and fragile. Let's face it, Sarah, you and I are the type that would never get away with it.'

'Thank God for that,' Sarah replied cheerfully. 'Women like that get up my nose, and I know I couldn't keep it up for more than a day.'

'Bed?' Samantha asked uncertainly.

'Swim first, then a shower and bed, and I shall put a "Do Not Disturb" notice on my door.'

'A swim is a good idea. The air's still very humid, and it might be relaxing.' Samantha changed into a bikini and wrapped a large beach towel round her waist. She was tired, but she knew she would not sleep if she went straight to bed now.

As they lazily swam the length of the pool, Samantha was able to think clearly. Laurie Martin, or rather Lorenzo Martinello, as he had been all day, had reacted as a small boy would have done when caught stealing apples. He had reached out for something that attracted him, prepared to enjoy it, now that his beloved was away, as he thought for ever, but had been sharply brought back into line by Caterina's sudden return; expected to jump to her slightest request and to be there to meet her, even in the middle of the night, and to accompany her in the ambulance, when there must be very efficient attendants—and of course her husband, who nobody had as yet mentioned, must be with her.

Laurie knew that Samantha was forbidden fruit, even if Caterina had no time for him as a husband, she thought. Did this mean that he must never marry, but must trail along in her scented wake, to be a kind of pet, taken up when wanted and put away when other more exciting or richer people appeared?

Samantha splashed and tried a crawl. That was ridiculous. He was strong and self-willed and would never be tied to such a situation. She coughed out some water she had taken in when she sighed. Who am I fooling? she asked herself. If he was in love, he would be faithful for ever. Desire and his own virility might make him want a pretty woman from time to time, but his heart would be with the only one he chose to love.

'Sarah!' she said, spluttering as she collided with a fast-swimming body. '*Must* you?' She brushed the water from her eyes and pushed back her saturated hair.

'Sorry.' The deep, masculine voice sounded anything but sorry. 'It gets crowded about dawn. I thought I'd have the pool to myself, and yet I find two dolphins here before me. At least, I thought they were when I glimpsed them through the gloom, but dolphins don't wear bikinis and never mutter when they're swimming.'

Samantha trod water. 'What are you doing here?' she demanded.

'I'm staying here, if you remember. I live in the cottage,' Laurie explained politely. 'I came back for a swim, a rest and some breakfast.'

'You prefer Maria's omelettes after all?' She climbed out of the pool.

'Pity about that,' he said, as if the visit to see the fishing boats and breakfast at the waterside *trattoria* was nothing. 'See you at eight in the dining-room.'

'No, I shall be fast asleep. I don't want breakfast,' she said coldly, and rubbed her hair vigorously with the towel.

'You need to shampoo it. It'll be all spiky after this water,' Laurie told her. 'I don't know what they use as a pool purifier here, but it might turn your hair green, and I really don't fancy you as a punk.'

'You needn't look at it,' she replied sweetly, and walked quickly away to her room.

She took a strand of hair between her fingers and shrugged. He was right. After she had been in the pool before this swim she had showered and shampooed as routine. A reluctant smile betrayed her, and she was glad he wasn't there to see her capitulation as she used her most expensive shampoo and conditioner and felt clean and fragrant once more.

A sharp tap on her bedroom door woke her and she sat up, rubbing her eyes. Brilliant sunlight reflected in the mirror dazzled her, and for a moment she couldn't see who was standing in the doorway. Her almost transparent baby-doll pyjamas clung to her body and the flowers in the fabric made the pink and white of her breasts almost as flowerlike as the roses in the design.

'It's eight o'clock,' Laurie Martin said accusingly, and she hastily drew the sheet up over her chest. Her freshly washed hair glistened with health and tumbled over her eyes, and her lips and cheeks were pink with sleep. He stared at her for a full minute, then turned away and said curtly, 'Get dressed. We're late. I'll have coffee ready in five minutes, with a croissant if you really want it.'

'How dare you burst in here and order me about?' she snapped, more embarrassed than angry. 'I said I wanted to sleep.'

'And I asked you to be down ready for breakfast at eight,' he replied.

'You didn't ask. You assumed I'd do as you ordered,' she said. 'But I told you I intended sleeping late. I doubt if Sarah or Mark are conscious yet, are they?'

'I don't want them,' he said impatiently. 'I need your help. Didn't I explain?' Samantha sank down in the bed.

'There isn't time now. Get dressed,' he repeated, then went out and closed the door.

'"Please, Samantha," would be nice,' she muttered, but she slipped out of bed and put on the first garment that came to her hand, a cream sundress with an appliquéd spray of flowers on the bodice. It was quick to put on as she could wear no bra under the slender shoulder-straps and she knew if the day was hot only bikini briefs under it would be possible to wear to keep reasonably cool.

Vigorously she brushed her hair and applied a light lipstick and moisturiser, but no eye make-up, as she sensed that a very impatient man was waiting in the dining-room. He had sounded as if they might be going away from the villa, so she grabbed her bag and holdall, with a jacket that matched the dress and a visor of cream linen.

Laurie pointed to the full cup of coffee. 'I said we'd be there at nine,' he said. 'Traffic's building up as Amalfi is full of visitors after yesterday's procession and regatta.'

'Be where at nine?' Samantha asked politely but with a visible trace of annoyance.

'At the clinic, of course!'

She sat down and carefully buttered a croissant as if she had all day to do it. 'Oh, what's happening there? Is Jenny being discharged and you want me to bring her back to the hostel? Surely a taxi would do. Taxis are very useful to transport females who are no longer wanted.' She bit the end of the crisp pastry. 'Does she have to be pushed out this early in the day to make room for unexpected emergencies?'

Laurie reddened. 'It's true that Jenny's coming out this morning. She's well enough now and can rest at the hostel, or even stay here if necessary.'

'I thought she was staying for a few more days,' Samantha said. 'Did someone need the bed and she had to leave to make room for the new patient?' she asked again as she sensed that he had avoided that part of her question.

'That's right. You know how it is—beds are scarce and emergencies take priority.'

'*Real* emergencies do,' Samantha agreed.

'Caterina had to come back to see Sir Ralph,' he said as if that were all she needed to know.

'How did it go?' she asked.

'How did what go?'

'The operation. It has been done, I suppose? I assume that she was diagnosed in Geneva and flown here for an emergency op.' She looked up. 'But if she was all that urgently in need of surgery they'd never have risked letting her come here by air. So I assume her condition is the same now as when she was married, and, as it's been diagnosed by a surgeon as a condition that wouldn't respond to medical treatment, this became a routine operation that could be done at any time.'

Laurie sat down. 'Caterina wanted to come back at once,' he said.

'In the middle of the night, upsetting the arrangements of dozens of people?' Samantha yawned. 'Robbing weary revellers of their sleep?'

'You will help?' His voice was lower and pleading.

'Help? Nobody's told me what I'm expected to do.'

'Scrub for her operation, of course,' Laurie explained as if amazed that she had not read his mind.

'I've never met Caterina and I don't know what's been found on examination, so I can't pretend to be an interested party, especially as Sir Ralph has told me that I'm not to work in a theatre until I return to

London. The clinic is well staffed, so what's the problem? Is it really urgent?'

He glanced at her polite but frozen expression, then looked away. 'They think she has a small ovarian cyst and possibly salpingitis that would account for the pain. A laparoscopy will show up what it's like, and they can deal with it by keyhole surgery.'

'Not urgent,' Samantha said flatly. 'I could have stayed in bed and it could have waited a day or so.'

'She wanted it done quickly once she knew she'd have just three small cuts in her abdomen—one for the laparoscope and the others to line up and introduce the instruments and operate. She was dreading being scarred by a big incision.'

'I don't see your problem,' Samantha said. 'It sounds routine, and with the staff there they can cope without me.'

'The theatre superintendent is off duty and the theatre was cleared yesterday as no surgical list had been arranged, so they're short-staffed,' Laurie explained.

'If it isn't any more urgent than on the day of the wedding, why not wait for a day when the theatre's working normally?'

'Sir Ralph will be here for a day or so, but I have to be back at Beattie's tomorrow, and she wants to see me after the op.'

'Is her husband with her?' queried Samantha. 'Surely he's the one to tell her that all's well after the operation?'

'He came with her,' he admitted. 'But Paolo hates hospitals and asked me to go with him.'

'Are you good friends?' she asked. It didn't tie up
with the way that Laurie had spoken when he
watched the bridal couple walk down the steps of
the cathedral, as if Paolo must be completely unac-
ceptable as a bridegroom or might even be a
monster.

'Paolo? We grew up together, with Caterina and
another family. He's fine, but not the man for
Caterina. He dominates her one minute, insisting
that she does as he wants, as he did over this business
until he was proved wrong, and then indulges her
shamelessly the next.'

'From what I hear, he sounds a good choice and
one that many girls would envy, and I'm sure
Caterina can wind him round her little finger if she
really wants something,' said Samantha.

He looked at her sharply. 'Someone has been
discussing Caterina with you.' She made no reply.
'Someone who knows only half the picture,' he
added soberly.

'Well, I'm not permitted to work as I take orders
from Sir Ralph in this, as his guest and as his future
junior theatre sister, but maybe I won't go back to
bed, I'll just convalesce on the terrace,' she said.

'Stay there,' he commanded, and went to the
telephone. A minute later he called, and she went
to take the receiver from his rigidly held hand.

'Samantha? How are you feeling?' Sir Ralph
asked. Her heart sank. 'I wonder if you could help.
I know I wanted you to rest as much as possible and
enjoy Amalfi, but we're in a bit of a spot, and you
do have clear throat swabs now.'

'Very well,' she replied. 'If *you* want me to help, Sir Ralph, obviously I'll do my best.'

'Good girl. It won't take more than an hour, and then Laurie can take you out for a nice lunch somewhere.'

'Not if I can avoid it,' she murmured as she put down the receiver. *Men*! They took what they wanted, gave you a pat on the head in the shape of a promised lunch, then forgot.

'It seems my convalescence is over,' she said, without a smile. 'I can't refuse Sir Ralph's request, so what do you want me to bring?'

'Just a clean hanky and a smile,' Laurie said. 'The rest is in the car.'

'I'll get my purse, in case I have to find my own way back by taxi, and a clean hanky,' she said. 'That's the easy part.'

'I'm sorry about last night,' Laurie said, with a sideways look at her stony face.

'It wasn't the best way to end a wonderful day,' she shrugged, 'but it was all a matter of your priorities. You were summoned to go and you went. I understand perfectly.'

'I don't think you do.' He drove in silence, and they soon reached the clinic.

A porter was waiting to take any baggage they had brought, and Samantha was shown into a pleasant room where a series of lockers showed that the regular staff used it for a changing-room. A girl pointed to a row of theatre boots and white shoes and handed her a thin plastic apron, then laughed.

'Oh, no!' Samantha realised too that she couldn't take off her sundress without being naked from the

waist up. 'Theatre pyjamas?' she asked hopefully,
and the girl tried several of the locker doors to see if
someone had left a set of female theatre clothes,
then she shrugged and went away and brought a pair
of loose trousers and a huge short-sleeved shirt that
were obviously the property of a tall man. Over this
baggy gear, Samantha tied the apron, and felt as if
she needed a second belt to tie the excess folds of
the trousers firmly in some order. She found a pair
of white shoes to fit, so she didn't have to disappear
completely in theatre boots as well as the ill-fitting
garments.

Sir Ralph chuckled. His pyjamas fitted well and
even his disposable theatre cap looked smart. 'You'll
have to grow a little, my dear,' he said. 'Good of
you to help out. She's a tiresome girl, but we do our
best.'

Samantha's annoyance faded. It wasn't his fault
that Caterina had descended on the clinic and
demanded attention. He was the completely professional surgeon who had agreed to do whatever
was necessary when the right diagnosis was made.

'We scrub here,' he said. 'She's with the anaesthetist in there, and Laurie's having a word before she
goes under anaesthetic. Ah, there he is. We can get
cracking. Just you and me and Laurie to do this one,
and a girl to pick up swabs who speaks no English,
so Laurie's invaluable on several counts.'

Samantha saw the incredulous glance that Laurie
gave her and wished her cap and mask hid even
more of her face. The glamour of hospital uniform?
Forget it, she told herself firmly, and checked her
instrument trolley. She counted the swabs in the

packets of ten and nodded to the girl, indicating that
there were in fact ten in each pack, then arranged
the instruments in the order in which they would be
used, pleased to find that Sir Ralph had brought his
own bag of tools, with which every nurse who had
worked with him at Beattie's in London was familiar, if only in a junior capacity when they cleaned
them!

Crisply folded sterile towels were ready to edge
the site of operation, but first Samantha handed a
long-handled swab holder with a swab dipped in
acriflavine to the surgeon. Laurie spoke to the girl
in Italian and Sir Ralph paused with the swab
halfway to the exposed skin. 'Sorry, sir, I just asked
if they had any skin paint that was less staining than
flavine, but she said no.'

'I always use this, or mercurochrome, which is
even brighter,' Sir Ralph said firmly. 'I like to see
where I'm cutting and know I've purified the skin
properly.' He sniffed audibly. 'I suppose Caterina
would like pale blue to match her nightie. You can
tell her it will fade to a nice pale mud colour in
time.'

'I know,' Laurie said with feeling.

Sir Ralph made a tiny incision through which he
passed the long laparoscope, a telescope to view the
inside of the abdomen. Laurie sealed off a few
bleeding points with laser, and when asked peered
down the tube to the bright light showing the cyst.
'Benign?' he asked.

'As blameless as a baby, I'd say, but we'll have it
out and send it for section.'

'Are you going to look further?' Laurie asked.

'Might as well take a look at her Fallopian tubes,' Sir Ralph said, shifting the angle of the inspecting laparoscope. He whistled softly. 'Nasty bit of inflammation here. The right tube is stuck down, and it looks as if this is a very old infection.'

'Five years?' There was agony in Laurie's voice.

'Why five?' Sir Ralph asked quietly. 'What do you know about this?'

'Her family have no idea,' Laurie said in a warning voice.

'Come on, man, I can't stay here all day with this thing inside her while you make dark statements. She's my patient, and I don't give a damn what she got up to at that finishing school in Switzerland five years ago.'

'You knew?' demanded Laurie.

'She did tell me of the discomfort and I knew it must have been an infection that had left adhesions,' Sir Ralph explained, 'but when she refused to have a thorough examination and said she wanted to do as Paolo suggested—be treated by fringe methods— I knew she was hiding something. The growing cyst put pressure on certain nerves and pushed the tube out of place, and then the whole side began to be painful because of the tension.'

'What do you propose?' Samantha turned to her trolley and made a quick check of swabs, although no swab could be lost in that tiny incision. They seemed to have forgotten that she heard every word, and she wished she was far away and need never know what they had found.

'Tell me the whole story while I get the cyst out,' Sir Ralph said. 'Sucker, Nurse. Quite a bit of free fluid here. Ah, that's better. Now the long snippers and forceps through the other incision, and have the laser ready to seal the stump of the cyst. Hold the laparoscope, Doctor. Right—just there.'

A minute later a small cyst about the size of a golf ball was pulled through the incision, a tight fit, but it came away without rupturing. Samantha put it carefully in a sterile kidney dish and kept it on the trolley in case the girl threw it away.

'I have to enlarge the incision slightly, but I'll do my best to leave no lasting scar,' Sir Ralph said. 'Scalpel, Nurse.'

Samantha mopped a few beads of blood from the site and watched as the surgeon carefully probed and cut with the remote-control forceps and knife. 'Suck and seal,' he ordered from time to time. 'Ask him if she's all right at his end and say this is taking a little more time than I'd reckoned.'

Laurie spoke to the anaesthetist, who nodded and adjusted one output of gas and gave Caterina more curare to relax the abdominal muscles. The monitors showed that her respirations were even and strong, and her pulse-rate was normal.

Laurie took a deep breath. 'Caterina went to that school and did well until she fell in love and became pregnant. The whole idea of the school was to prevent anything like that happening. Parents wanted to feel they could sleep at night knowing they'd pushed their responsibilities on to firm shoulders and that their girls were safe from the seamy side of life and sex. A crowd of very nubile girls must be difficult to watch all the time, and discipline was lax. The girls were allowed out with brothers, cousins and friends of the family.'

'Who did the abortion?' Sir Ralph asked.

'The boy arranged it with a doctor he knew in Germany, and they pretended to be visiting relatives in Bonn for the half-term holiday. When Caterina came back, she had a fever which they put down to food poisoning, but she wouldn't allow an examination by the doctor from the local hospital who treated anything medical or surgical that occurred at the finishing school. It all blew over, and the boy responsible left Geneva.'

'Did she never give a hint to anyone?'

'She admitted it to me when I wanted her to have a thorough examination, but she still refused to be examined until the homoeopath very wisely told her bluntly that if she didn't have it cleared up she might be in for real trouble,' Laurie explained.

'The little madam!' Sir Ralph's disapproval was mixed with grudging admiration. 'Once she was safely married, she could relax, especially as Paolo doesn't think much of us medics as a breed.' He laughed. 'We can tell him there was an ovarian cyst and we had to take out the Fallopian tube on that side as there were adhesions. All perfectly true, and my own remarks and opinions can stay in my head.'

'Will you look at the other tube, sir?' Laurie sounded anxious.

'I have. It's healthy and the other ovary is in good working order, so she can have babies, if that's what she wants.'

'You'll tell her that, sir?'

'Of course—unless you'd like to have that pleasant duty?'

'No, thank you. I've been involved quite enough. I'm glad it's all over and she's able to have a normal married life, but I hope they make their home in Geneva and not in Amalfi,' Laurie said with feeling.

Samantha saw the tension in the broad shoulders and knew that Dr Lorenzo Martinello was under stress. Of course he wanted Caterina to live far away so that the sight of her in all her loveliness couldn't haunt him, and taunt him with the knowledge that he could never possess her.

'Swabs correct,' Samantha said clearly, and handed a fresh swab dipped in more flavine to the surgeon, who carefully dabbed the bright dye all over the small scars that had been sutured with degradable gut in the subcutaneous tissue under the skin to avoid scars.

'Tell Sister to get her out of bed this evening, and she must sit out tomorrow and do exercises,' Sir Ralph said firmly. 'No lying in bed as a fragile invalid. She can go home in three days' time.' He cut into the cyst in the kidney dish and then into the tissue of the Fallopian tube, while Laurie put a light dressing on the wounds and went with the patient to the ward.

'Is it all right?' Samantha asked.

'Yes, but I'll send it for section.' He thought for a moment. 'Laurie can take it to the path lab at Beattie's tomorrow. Safer that way. Here, everyone knows everything that happens, and we might as well keep this a private case in all senses of the word.'

Samantha cleared the trolley and left the girl to wash the instruments and put them away in Sir Ralph's case. She went to the locker-room and showered, glad to be in her own cool sundress again. A nurse called her to go to the surgeons' room for coffee, and she went with some reluctance.

Laurie was sprawled over a low armchair, still dressed in pyjama bottoms, his brown skin almost golden in the sunlight and the lines of his body relaxed but strong and firm. Samantha looked away. He loved Caterina, and would never need an ordinary English nurse as a wife or lover.

'Wait for me,' he said, as soon as he saw she was ready to leave. 'Drink your coffee, and I'll be ready in ten minutes after I've been down to the ward again.'

'Don't hurry,' she said sweetly. 'Take all the time you need.'

'You'll wait?'

'I'll have coffee and then do some shopping,' she told him. 'Caterina will be awake now and might need you to stay with her. I really don't want to waste any more time here. I'll go back to the villa by taxi.'

The shower in the surgeons' cubicle stopped jetting water and a rather damp surgeon put out an arm for his cup of coffee. Sir Ralph had a huge towel draped round his waist as he sank into a plastic chair. 'Good!'. He sipped with enjoyment. 'That first cup after surgery really hits the spot. Taking Samantha to lunch?' he asked, as if it was a settled fact.

'No, she says not,' Laurie said with an annoyed

glance at the crisply dressed girl who refused to look at him.

'I have some shopping to do and then an afternoon by the pool, I think,' Samantha said. 'Good morning, gentlemen.' She walked away with her head held high, determined that Dr Laurie Martin would never see that he meant anything to her ever again.

CHAPTER EIGHT

'THOUGHT I'd say goodbye.' Samantha smiled as soon as she heard Carol's voice. 'Just off to Singapore. Luciano is livid,' she added cheerfully. 'He has another two days off and threatens to take a lover, or to make me pregnant the next time we meet in two weeks' time, so I'm here when he wants me all the time, the male chauvinist!'

'Would that be bad?' laughed Samantha.

'I need another year,' Carol said firmly. 'Too many people marry and start families, then find they haven't time to talk to each other. The women stay at home and the men go out with the lads and they drift apart. I love Luciano and I want him to stay faithful.' She laughed. 'Anything I can bring back for you from the Far East?'

'I shan't be here for much longer, so we may not meet for ages. Leave it until we meet in London.'

'Will you be bored now that I've left and Lorenzo is back in England?'

'He's gone?' Samantha found her throat tightening as it had done after her tonsillectomy.

There was silence for a moment on the other end of the line, then Carol said rather cautiously, 'He left this morning, and asked me to say goodbye to you as his plane left before you'd be awake.' Carol waited for a reply that didn't come, then added, 'That man's so infuriating, Samantha. I think he·

believes he's upset you and he's too proud to do anything about it.'

'That's not true.' Samantha managed a forced laugh. 'We met by accident and events threw us together, but he's gone now, and I doubt if he'll give me another thought. I suppose I've been quite useful to him, and at the revels we found a certain mutual attraction, but he doesn't need my help now, or my company. He can concentrate on his other life. That's what will happen to both of us. He did say, when I mentioned that I might miss this place, that once I leave I shall become engrossed in my real life and the places and things I love and find more familiar. It will be like that for sure,' she insisted.

'You could have fooled me,' Carol said.

'How's Caterina?' Samantha asked politely.

'Fine. Lorenzo told Luciano she'll be going back to Geneva with her husband today, and after a few weeks they can have their real honeymoon. I don't know what Lorenzo and Sir Ralph said to her, but she's been very much more subdued and pleasant since the op. Last night, when Lorenzo saw her to say goodbye, she was as he remembered her, sweet and charming, and she looked completely well, and was very grateful to him for staying here an extra day or so when he was really due back in London.'

'Have a great time in Singapore, Carol,' said Samantha. 'You have my London address. Be sure to contact me when you can.'

Samantha picked up her beach towel and sunglasses and walked slowly down to the poolside patio. Laurie had left without saying goodbye. He had not been near her for the past two days and he must have known when he was leaving. He had managed to find time to say goodbye to Caterina last night. I don't go to bed that early! she thought. Even after seeing her, he could have contacted me. A brief phone call or a note under my door would have been something. Not enough, but at least it would have been a polite gesture.

Sarah was in the water. 'Hi,' she called. 'I'm getting out now, so stay dry until we've had coffee.' She erupted from the water and shook herself like a puppy. 'I think my boobs are getting bigger. What do you think?'

'I think you have a very good figure,' Samantha said. 'By next year you may want to slim down if you develop much more,' she added in a teasing voice. 'If you take up catering and sample all your baking you might well end up like Maria, and they'll never let you wear that dreamy outfit at the next lot of revels.'

'You're a bitch,' Sarah told her with a smile. 'Let's go shopping this afternoon. Jenny's better and she wants a few things, so if you'll drive, we can take her with us.'

'I'll ask Maria for coffee,' Samantha said. Before she had met Laurie Martin, this would have been the pattern of her days at the Villa Stresa. Visits to places of interest and to the many fascinating shops in the area, maybe a trip to Pompeii and Herculaneum and a boat ride to Capri would have been the highlights of the holiday, and she would have returned to London refreshed and full of the stimulating memories of this beautiful part of Italy.

Slow down, she told herself, and took a deep

breath. The affair that had never got started was over and the world was still beautiful, but its beauty saddened her and left an ache in her heart as she drove along the winding coast road and listened to the bright chatter of the two girls and Mark, who had decided to go with them.

The next day seemed long, and even the blue sky and the deep azure sea did nothing to lift her spirits. Suddenly she ached for a dull day with damp air and the sight of red London buses. She picked up a book of poetry and read, half smiling. Rupert Brooke had felt as she did.

'God! I will pack, and take a train, And get me to England once again!'

Other images haunted her as she read the poems and she tried to take a siesta, but she grew hotter and hotter until she decided to swim again. Sir Ralph had gone, and even Nathan had gone to explore Tuscany, leaving the younger members of the language school at the hostel, none of them great for company.

So much and yet so little had happened to change her life in the time that she had been at the villa, and she had two more weeks of loneliness to bear, in paradise.

'Samantha?' Sarah sounded breathless. 'Phone for you,' she called.

Samantha draped her towel round her waist and ran to the hallway. Guido's family had suggested a barbecue, and this was probably the call to arrange it. She smiled. Guido was not comfortable on the telephone with his fractured English; and I'm not much better with my Italian, she thought.

'Samantha? This is Ralph Gower. I rang my daughter and she wants to come home for a while. Says it's getting far too hot in Amalfi, and I wondered if you ought to get out too.'

'I'm fine, Sir Ralph,' she said. 'The pool makes such a difference when we get hot.'

'You're feeling really fit now?' he asked. She assured him that she felt better than she had felt for months. 'Good—that's very good. Now I wonder if I could ask a very great favour?' She smiled, knowing Sir Ralph usually got what he wanted through charm and consideration. 'My theatre sister in my Harley Street clinic has been rushed off to have a rather nasty fracture reduced—an unfortunate clash with a bus in Regent Street. I'm left without a familiar pair of hands that I can trust, and I have several private cases that can't wait until I come back from a congress in Switzerland next month.'

'Can't you do them in the private block in the Princess Beatrice, sir?' she asked.

'I've already asked them and they're agreeable, but they're short-staffed owing to holidays and a few slight cases of odd infections like tonsillitis, through stress and examination fever! By the way,' he added casually, 'I saw the final exam results, which will be in the post shortly, and of course, as we all knew would happen, you've passed with flying colours. You're now officially able to take the post of theatre sister.'

'That's wonderful!' exclaimed Samantha. 'I didn't expect to hear until next month.'

'You still don't know anything, so keep quiet about it for the present! I have prior knowledge as one of the examiners, and I took a peep as I also have a vested interest in your results. Will you fly back tomorrow with Sarah and take the rest of your leave after I've gone to Switzerland?'

'What can I say? What about seats in a plane? This is the busy period for travel.'

'You'll come? I knew you would,' he said with satisfaction. 'Everything's arranged. A friend with a private jet is leaving tomorrow at nine-thirty a.m. He has room for you and Sarah, and I've told her the details.'

'Do they know at Beattie's that I'm coming back?' Her brain seemed in a whirl.

'Everything laid on, my dear, and I'm very grateful to you. By the way, you're welcome to go back to the villa to finish your holiday—with a plane ticket at my expense, of course,' Sir Ralph said.

I've passed! I'm through the exams and I can take that job in the theatre! Elation drove away Samantha's depression and she laughed softly. Whatever happened now, she had a good career in front of her, and to hell with all men!

'Sarah?' she called. 'Do you really want to go back home? I thought you loved it here.'

'I'm bored. Mark's with Jenny most of the time and Rhoda's a misery now that Nathan has escaped from her clutches, and you've been going about with a face as long as a fiddle, as my granny says, so why not go home? At least I have a few friends there and something to do other than lie in the sun. I want to go riding, and a girl from college has a boat at

Hamble where we can stay for a week or so and do some studying. She's a bit of an egghead, so I might, just might, do some real work with her, and she's just the kind of girl my parents approve of, so I shall be safe from all temptations.'

'Well, we'd better pack our gear,' Samantha said.

'You're coming too? Great! So he managed it? My dad is the most devious man I know,' Sarah said, laughing.

'I'm sure you'll meet many more who are good at getting their own way, but they may lack Sir Ralph's charm.' Samantha looked at the blue sky and felt a pang of unease. Some men had more charm even than Sir Ralph and then could leave a girl with a badly bruised ego and a lasting sadness.

'We'll pack most of our stuff and then have a last pasta at the *trattoria*. Maria will be furious, as she usually packs a great box of cakes for me to take back, and she won't have the time now to do more than weep over us tomorrow morning.'

'Finished?' Samantha asked later.

'More or less.' Sarah kicked a bulging squashy bag that looked ready to burst, but the zip held firm. 'I didn't think I'd brought much this time, but I seem to have loads of extra clothes. I need another bag, so I'll pinch one from Dad's suite. He won't know, and he can bring it back the next time he comes over. Mark's a sod! He says I must take back all my books as he refuses to carry them when he leaves next week.' Sarah sighed. 'I wish I'd got some man to fall for me as he has for Jenny. She can flutter her eyelids and he'll carry all her books and everything.

He's only going back next week because she's going then.'

Samantha laughed. 'You're lucky to have a brother who's been a friend for so long. Mark's a nice guy, and even if he falls for Jenny he'll never really neglect you. You're far too close, and in any case you like Jenny and can stay friends.'

Sarah made a face. 'Great! I just love playing gooseberry to those two. Come on, we'll put the bags in the hall and go down to the village. I must buy some fresh Parmesan in a lump, to take back. It's cheaper here and much, much better than the tiny packets I buy back home. Laurie likes it too, so you'd better get some.'

'I don't think I'll bother. I doubt if Laurie and I will be seeing each other again except perhaps on duty.'

'Don't be daft!' said Sarah. 'Ring him up as soon as you get back and invite him for supper. Tagliatelle and loads of grated Parmesan should lure him as quickly as any mouse.'

'I don't like mice,' Samantha said shortly. 'And he can buy his own cheese.'

She bought two bottles of the smooth local wine, and hesitated as Sarah chose a huge piece of Parmesan cheese. 'I like it, too, and it's quite cheap compared to the same kind of cheese in England,' Samantha admitted, as if justifying her purchase, and she bought a piece as well.

They didn't get as far as the *trattoria* that evening as Maria refused to let them go away without a huge Italian supper of antipasto, cannelloni, lamb with herbs, and almond cake. 'I hope they don't put us on the scales as well as the luggage,' sighed Sarah as they trudged upstairs to bed feeling rather too full. Samantha knew she wouldn't sleep unless she had some fresh air, so she fetched a light jacket and wandered by the pool, in the dark.

'Goodbye,' she murmured. 'Goodbye, Villa Stresa and Amalfi.' Lights from the road far below glimmered and changed as first the red tail-lights of traffic glowed and then the white headlights took over as the traffic lights changed, as if strings of rubies and diamonds moved endlessly through the night.

The soft air stirred her hair, like the gentle kiss of a man who was half in love with her, wanted her body and yet was bound by love to another woman.

'It's time to leave,' she told the scented trees. 'Time to forget this place and everything I grew to love here.'

She passed the kitchen window and smelled the fragrance of herbs and tomatoes, and tears came to her eyes. Maria gave love in the form of food and good cooking, and it was a good kind of love, but tomorrow there would not even be that care left as the plane flew high over the Bay of Naples and jetted back home.

'There's Vesuvius,' Sarah said as the plane circled and found its path across the sea. She laughed. 'Each time I come here I swear I'll climb it, but as yet I haven't been any further than Pompeii. Next time you come we'll put on boots and go to the crater.'

'Next time? I don't think I shall ever see Pompeii

now,' Samantha said sadly. 'I'd planned so much, but here I am, going home again without doing half of what I planned.'

'You'll be back,' Sarah said with conviction. 'They all like you. You fit in well, and you've cut your holiday short just because my domineering father beckoned, and you were too polite to say no.'

'I wanted to go home,' Samantha told her. 'I have work to do and friends to visit.' Already she looked forward to working with Sir Ralph again. She told herself firmly that she must plan her life carefully to fill up the dark places of loneliness that might surface if she allowed herself to remember Lorenzo Martinello.

He was two people—the passionate Italian who had held her close and murmured endearments in her ear, as they danced with their bodies moulded as one, in love and deepening desire; and the more reserved English doctor with the dark blue eyes and quirky humour, who was fun, and yet as dangerous as Lorenzo, when she remembered the sensual touch of his hands on her shoulders and his lips brushing hers.

The plane landed well on time, and the two girls looked out at the sunlit tarmac. Light clouds hung against a pale blue sky and the air was soft as they walked into the main building to claim their luggage that still had to pass through Customs. They heard the Tannoy calling one late passenger to fill a plane due to leave.

Another flight was called for Geneva, and Samantha looked up sharply as she recalled that Caterina would now be back in Switzerland with her husband. As if in another world, passengers flowed past barriers on the other side of the lounge, the ones coming from hot climates bronzed, their clothes crumpled and a bit grubby, and the others getting away from the cool weather in England, with pale faces and looking very tidy in fresh holiday clothes.

Businessmen with briefcases marched to the gate for club passengers on the Geneva plane—and Samantha gasped. One man stood out from the rest. He carried a flight bag and a newspaper and wore a suit of continental cut. He was in a hurry as he caught up with the last of the passengers and showed his boarding pass.

'That's Laurie!' Sarah exclaimed, and waved, unable to get closer as a barrier divided those coming from those about to leave, but the dark-haired man went away through the door and away from the airport lounge. 'I thought for a moment he'd come to meet us, but he's leaving England again,' Sarah said with an air of disappointment. She laughed. 'Caterina really does make everyone jump when she wants attention. I bet he's off to Geneva to see her. Doesn't she ever let go?'

Samantha felt vaguely sick. She told herself it was delayed air-sickness, but her heart told her she was no closer to forgetting Laurie than she had been in Amalfi.

'Taxi for me, and I suppose another for you, as we go in different directions,' Sarah said when they arrived by train at Victoria Station.

'I think I'll have a cup of station coffee first,' Samantha decided.

'Not for me.' Sarah turned up her nose. 'Be sure

to come to my eighteenth birthday party. I'll send a
formal invitation as soon as they're printed. Mark
refused to have a real party, but I want the whole
works. Dad's doing me proud, and I want the world
to know that Sarah Gower's really grown up at last
and ready for life with a capital "L." Who knows? I
might meet a famous film director who'll cast me in
a fabulous film.'

'What happened to catering college?' asked
Samantha.

'I'll do that as well, or until I'm discovered.' Sarah
gave her a quick hug. 'Be happy,' she said, and
vanished in the direction of the taxi queue, leaving
Samantha to a plastic cup of hot coffee, the station
and the pigeons.

The huge double gates of the Princess Beatrice
Hospital stood wide open as they did all day and
every day, rather like relics of the portcullis of an
ancient castle, but instant access to the casualty
department and Outpatients was essential at all
times, and even the old retired porter Claud, who
still came to see his friends among the porters in
Casualty, couldn't recall a time when the gates were
shut, not even during the war. He swore that it was
only the cunning of the hospital governor that had
saved the gates from being melted down to make
bombers for World War Two.

Samantha went to the lodge to see if there was
any mail for her that hadn't been sent on to Amalfi,
but really to make sure that Dr Laurie Martin had
not left a message for her. Maybe in the flat, she
thought when the porter handed her only junk mail,

and she dragged her luggage up the hill to the flat in the block rented out to nurses and doctors working at the hospital.

Thankfully she dropped her two bags on the bed and eased her shoulders back before going down again to the small office where lettered partitions held mail addressed to the occupants of the house. Her heart missed a beat. A handwritten note with no postage stamp rested in her pigeon-hole. She took it eagerly, then her eyes lost their gleam as she saw that it was from Sir Ralph Gower and not from Laurie.

Welcome back. Sorry to rush you, but can you take Theatre C at five tonight? I've told them to prepare, and my bag of tricks is ready up there. As I usually bring my own staff for private work you'll be accepted as routine, but tomorrow you ought to make your return known so you don't lose your holiday time.

Samantha glanced at her watch. A quick late lunch and a shower was all that she could now fit into the day before going up to the theatre at four-thirty to make sure that all was ready for the operation. She ate the sandwiches she had bought in a kiosk at Victoria Station and made coffee, then unpacked and sorted out clothes for washing and some for dry-cleaning. She held the Italian dress up to her cheek, wondering if she would ever wear it again. It now seemed very chic, very foreign and totally beautiful, and she hung it up carefully before changing into a white uniform dress and cap and low-heeled white shoes.

Her hair was unruly and had grown a little while she had been away, showing no sign of wanting to be pinned down under the tiny cap, so she put on a wide Alice band of white Lycra as if about to play tennis, then put the cap on that. She walked across the car park, wearing her thick cloak as the wind was chill, and once inside the building she smelled the unforgettable smell of a hospital corridor. It's as if I'd never been away, she decided, and as if to make this even more definite a passing nurse called, 'Hello, Croft. I thought you were going away. When do you leave?'

'What it is to be missed,' Samantha murmured as she pushed open the swing doors leading to the anaesthetic-room of Theatre C.

She glanced at the blackboard on which the operations for the day were noted. Three were crossed out and had been done during the morning. 'Five p.m., laparoscopy and query hysterectomy,' she read. 'Private patient wing, Mrs Constance Webster.'

From the sterilising-room she heard the busy clatter that told her of the preparations for operation number four and saw the porter bring a heavy case of intravenous blood and bags of saline glucose into the theatre. She changed into theatre clothes and tied her mask firmly over her face before venturing into the sterilising-room.

'Staff Nurse Croft! You don't know how glad I am to see you! I began to think I'd have to scrub, and I'm not really ready for anyone as high-powered as Sir Ralph yet.' The second-year nurse smiled. 'The drums of sterile instruments are ready and I've laid

up two trolleys ready for you to arrange them before
you scrub.'

'Have you her history? What do we expect to
find?' Samantha asked. 'Trouble, from the look of
the intravenous trolley.'

'Sir Ralph wanted to get this operation over as
she's lost a lot of blood over the past three weeks
and is badly in need of more, but while her fibroids
go on bleeding there's no way of making the blood
stay put,' the nurse said.

'Has she had blood in the ward?' Samantha asked.

'She's on a blood drip now and we have enough
for the operation and for when she goes back to
Recovery or Intensive Care, whichever she needs.'

While they talked, Samantha was putting out all
the instruments she thought Sir Ralph might need.
'Put a Gossett's self-retaining retractor in to boil,'
she said. 'This is too big. I'll keep it on the trolley,
but I know he prefers the other lighter one if the
patient isn't too fat.' She put sutures in a kidney dish
and two needle-holders on the trolley. 'Good, I see
you've put out two packs of big muslin abdominal
packs. Put six more small Spencer Wells forceps in
the steriliser, as I'll need them to put on the ends of
the tapes so that we don't lose a pack inside the
abdomen.'

'I know we do that as a safety measure, Nurse,
but is it really necessary?' queried the other nurse.

'We don't know the patient or if she has fresh
blood in her abdominal cavity,' Samantha explained.
'Once I saw a large swab saturated with blood that
suddenly made it look really small enough to be a
blood clot and the same colour as the tissues. A pair

of forceps on the end of each tape hanging outside
the cavity makes sure that there are no accidents.
You'll keep a good swab count, Nurse? If she's as ill
as I think she must be, we don't want to hang about
while you sort out swabs and keep the patient
waiting with a hole in her middle that should be
stitched up quickly to reduce surgical shock as much
as possible!'

'I'm glad you're here, Nurse Croft. The registrar
shouts at me and I lose my cool and fumble with
things,' the nurse confessed.

'Don't worry. Sir Ralph never shouts unless
there's something dangerously wrong, and he stops
any aggro from his team,' Samantha laughed. 'By
the way, I hope you have his own pyjamas laid out
with the extra-thin plastic apron and size nine boots?
He's a vain man and likes to look like Dr Kildare!'

Voices from the scrubbing bay made her glance
quickly over the trolleys to see that everything was
in place, then she left the nurse to cover each one
with a sterile towel and went to join the surgeon and
his registrar.

Sir Ralph nodded to her, his eyes over the green
mask friendly and welcoming, and as the steam from
the elbow-operated taps clouded the highly polished
tiled walls as the team scrubbed Samantha felt as if
she had never been away.

The first incision was made, and the sucker hissed
away the blood before the bleeding points were
sealed. The theatre was quiet, as everyone there
concentrated on making speed safely, and Samantha
knew Sir Ralph was happy, doing the work he

enjoyed and having the help of Beattie's most famous anaesthetist, Dr Boris Pilatzcech.

Dr Boris checked the monitors and injected more relaxing drugs into the intravenous tubing so that the abdominal muscles didn't contract and make access to the cavity difficult. The fibroids were far too big to be removed by keyhole surgery, and at last the hugely distorted uterus was exposed and removed, the cervix sutured and the bleeding stopped for ever.

'How is she, Boris? Mind if I take a look at her tubes?'

'You can have another twenty minutes,' the calm voice said. 'She's doing fine, and her blood-pressure is levelling.'

Samantha watched, fascinated, as the surgeon slipped a finger under the right Fallopian tube and showed a badly scarred and useless organ which he removed, together with the ovary. 'The left side is healthy, and we want to leave the ovary to avoid trouble with her hormones later,' Sir Ralph told the young theatre nurse, who had tried to watch everything he did.

'Swab count?' asked the registrar.

'Correct, sir,' said the nurse, and Samantha stifled a smile as she saw how precisely the swabs had been spread out on the plastic sheet on the theatre floor so that there was no possibility of two being stuck together.

'Correct,' she agreed, having checked with the nurse the swabs left on the trolley. She handed Sir Ralph a needle-holder with the atraumatic needle and gut that he preferred for the delicate inner layers of tissue. He swabbed, stitched and tied, then stood back to look at the monitor screens, and grunted his satisfaction before cutting through the distended uterus and examining the many fibroids in the lining.

He did the same with the Fallopian tube while the registrar sewed the skin layer. 'Almost as bad as Caterina's,' Sir Ralph said quietly.

'She'll be all right, sir?'

'Both of them will be fine, but Caterina makes more fuss. She had a sudden whim for Laurie to fly out to Geneva to see her. Sweet child, but a handful, and Laurie can add nothing to what's been said to her husband unless she decides, very unwisely, to tell him the truth.'

Samantha handed the top dressing to the nurse and saw that the porters were waiting to take the patient back to her room as soon as Dr Boris gave the word and was ready to go with them. She walked with Sir Ralph to the surgeons' room, where coffee waited in vacuum flasks, hot and fresh and accompanied by sweet biscuits and slices of chocolate cake.

'Why shouldn't she tell her husband the truth?' Samantha asked.

'It would ruin her marriage,' Sir Ralph said. 'You don't know Paolo.' He stripped off his mask and poured coffee. 'There are some things a man like him can't take, and that's going to be the burden she must carry all her life. She must never tell him, or she'll lose him and all he can give her. Once the first child is born she'll forget the past and be secure, but until then she thinks she needs help from people like Laurie who've been close to her and her family.'

He looked at her with a searching gaze. 'Laurie

knows about her, and that allows her to talk about it
to him and so let off steam, and he thinks she should
now tell her husband the whole truth.'

'But is it fair to expect him to be at her beck and
call all the time?' she asked with some heat.

'He might not have gone to Geneva,' he replied
with a dismissive shrug.

'He went,' she said flatly. 'Sarah and I saw him
running to the flight gate.'

'Oh! That means she's frightened she'll tell Paolo
the truth. It must be a great temptation to unburden
herself, and she wants Laurie's moral support.'

'Until the next time,' Samantha said with a trace
of bitterness that made Sir Ralph look at her with
increased concern.

'I hope he'll be firm with her,' he said. 'I agree
that she expects too much, but you can help him,
Samantha.'

'Me?' she queried in disbelief.

'You.'

'I doubt if we shall meet again,' she began.

'The day after tomorrow, you're to scrub for me
again, and he'll be there,' he told her.

'If Caterina says so.'

'No, if I say so, and Laurie wants to be here, as I
know he will. He never shirks his duty, and he's a
damn good surgeon.'

'That's normal duty routine. I doubt if we shall
meet away from the hospital. We hardly know each
other, so I can't see where I'm concerned,' said
Samantha.

'You forget my crazy daughter and her eighteenth
birthday party.' He laughed. 'Yes, we shall all be

there—my family, Sarah's friends and you, with Carol if she's free, and Luciano and so many others that I shall never be able to retire for years as I shall be paying off the bills!'

Samantha bit her lip. 'I can't help him,' she said softly. He doesn't need any help. I'm the one who needs help, she thought.

'Boris! Have some coffee. You did a great job this afternoon and I'm indebted to you,' Sir Ralph said smoothly. 'How is she?'

Dr Boris sipped his coffee and smiled. 'Fine, but I'm going now. I've left her in good hands, and my wife will be livid if I don't get home for dinner. We have friends staying with us.'

Sir Ralph watched him go. 'I recall a time when Boris was the heart-throb of the entire hospital. He made a disastrous marriage which nearly destroyed him, and then Holly came along and tamed him with sweetness, and he's been happy ever after.' He laughed. 'Never underestimate the influence of love and a good woman,' he said. 'We may seem strong and macho, but we do love to be led by the nose at times. Looking back, I think my wife gets her own way all the time.'

'As Caterina leads men?' asked Samantha.

'As any woman can do if she really wants her own way, but a woman in love has a special power and can influence a man, especially if he loves her. Caterina should know she has nothing to fear from Paolo even if she doesn't stay quiet about the past.' His tone became brisk. 'I'll leave a message for Laurie and see you here tomorrow for two cases before the big one when he assists me in two days' time. You've really finished your contract here, as your training is over, and that gives you space to do private work for me until you take on a new agreement to work on the permanent staff as theatre sister.'

'You're going away, Sir Ralph?' asked Samantha.

'To the congress, and then you can take the rest of your holiday, and so can Laurie while he has a locum.'

'But not together,' she said firmly, and he smiled.

CHAPTER NINE

'I BROUGHT your invitation myself and I'm doing a round with them on my new bike.' Sarah laughed. 'Don't look so startled. I'm not pedalling all over London. I've got a motorbike—much better for traffic here than a car. I can weave a way through the traffic and get to places before the cars have even started.'

'What does Sir Ralph say about it?' Samantha asked.

'He was a bit off at first, but he can't talk! He had a bike when he was sixteen and burned up the racing circuits before he was married. I found a lot of old photographs of him looking very macho, and I showed them to him when he went all heavy about it.'

Samantha laughed. 'Difficult for the poor man, as he's such a great supporter of women's rights. Is that one of his cast-off leather jackets?'

'The trousers were too big, but this is perfect, and right back in fashion again.' Sarah chuckled. 'I can't think what his more stuffy colleagues would say if they knew about his past! I met Malcolm Readish in the car park before I took off my helmet, and he looked most disapproving and muttered something about disgusting women trying to be Hell's Angels. Maybe I'll wear this gear when he comes to dinner next week!'

'And maybe you won't!' Samantha said in a warning voice.

'No, not if I want a good party. You will be there?' Samantha nodded. 'Great. I have a few more to deliver to some of the junior doctors who are quite fun and some to the college.' Sarah wrinkled her nose. 'Difficult, as three have gone on a project and I'm not sure if they can get back in time. Oh, I wanted to ask you—where can I find Laurie?'

'I have no idea,' Samantha said.

'Brrr! Chilly in here,' Sarah remarked. 'Sounds as if he isn't flavour of the month.'

'It isn't that,' Samantha assured her, as if to lighten her cold response. 'I just don't know where he is. He came to the private theatre last week to assist with a very tricky operation on a woman with a bad prolapse and blocked Fallopian tubes, and we were all far too busy to exchange light conversation. After the op he stayed with the patient for a while in Recovery and didn't come back to the theatre.'

'So it's no use leaving the invitation with you?'

'Sir Ralph may know where to find him. Any others you want me to find for you?'

'Only this one. Dad's giving out his own now that he's back from the congress, but he said this man works at Beattie's sometimes and you met him in theatre.'

'Bruce Faulkner?' Samantha laughed. 'A real smoothy, but very good company. He was in Theatre the day when Sir Ralph and Laurie did that op. She was Dr Faulkner's private patient and he gowned up, but he didn't scrub as he's a physician and never touches a scalpel.'

'Dad says he wants to invite him and a couple more of his own friends in self-defence, as he says he'll be lost in a strident flood of teenagers unless he brings some opposition.'

'Bruce is nice,' Samantha said, and recalled the time after the operation when she had felt hot and sticky and very glad the case was over.

'I'd like to apologise for getting in the way,' Dr Faulkner had said as she put the last tray of instruments in the steriliser after they had been thoroughly cleaned.

'Thank you.' She had been surprised. Not many visitors who had caused so much trouble bothered to refer to it. He had stumbled against a trolley and put an unsterile, ungloved hand on it, which meant a swift transfer of the instruments to another sterile trolley.

'You were so kind,' he added. 'Most theatre sisters of my acquaintance would have made me feel like something bad the cat had left on the mat! But you made the change-over so quietly that even Sir Ralph didn't notice what was happening. I hate surgery,' he went on. 'I get nervous in the theatre and was glad when I became a physician and had no need to assist again.'

'Accidents happen,' she replied with a smile. Her cap, and the mask that now hung about her neck, were damp with the steam from the steriliser, and she felt grubby, but his hazel eyes were full of admiration and she warmed to him.

Laurie had nodded to her as he came from the scrubbing bay and saw her busy with the trolleys and checking her swabs, then he had been completely involved with the patient, who had shown signs of collapse and so added to the tension and the need to work fast and accurately.

Once, to her dismay, his hand had touched hers as she passed a pair of forceps to him, and even through the impersonal gloves she felt the same sensual magnetism that she had known in Amalfi, but he had firmly looked at the sucker in his hand and asked for another swab, showing no sign that he noticed the contact.

She changed and was ready to leave the theatre, with no further work for the day as she was still working privately for Sir Ralph. It was good to have time off and to ease herself back into work slowly after her convalescence before taking up her post as theatre sister at the famous Princess Beatrice Hospital, but now that she was back in London it seemed unimportant to take the rest of the holiday due to her. she found that Dr Faulkner was still in the surgeons' room, reading notes from his briefcase.

'Sir Ralph asked me to say goodbye and thank you, Sister, and he'll see you tomorrow. I stayed with Dr Martin to make sure that my patient recovered safely, then I came back here to read some notes in peace and quiet.' He packed away the papers and looked at his watch. 'Come on, I'll take you to lunch.' He smiled. 'You must be hungry after standing there for three hours, working hard.'

To her own surprise, Samantha found herself sitting in the Peregrine bar of the Falcon Inn eating *moules marinière* with a man who now seemed almost like an old friend. They talked easily, with none of the hang-ups of a couple with sexual tension between them, and Samantha had begun to wonder if this weren't the best relationship to have with a man—laughter and yet enough warmth to make the meeting close and intimate.

'Yes,' she said to Sarah, 'I'll take Bruce's invitation, as I shall see him this evening. I'm glad he's coming to the party—I began to think I'd be alone in a madding crowd.' She laughed. 'It's strange that when I was in Amalfi I thought I couldn't imagine life back here again, but now I enjoy my work and haven't had time to think of blue seas and wonderful scenery. I don't even want to go back when I have the rest of my leave.'

I'm safe, she thought. So long as I keep away from dangerous thoughts and dangerous emotions. I'm safe and calm, and Bruce is falling in love with me. I can handle that situation, and yet—who knows?— marriage to him might be the answer. A nice calm, uncomplicated marriage with enough affection to make it work, but no shattering heights or depths of passion, no trembling at a touch and no drowning in my own desire.

'Fine. See you soon.' Sarah pushed back her hair and slung her helmet over one arm. 'Do you think they'll let me in the common-room like this?'

'They'll be envious.' Samantha gave her an old-fashioned glance. 'You've invited Jeremy Bright, I hope? If all else fails you can talk engines, can't you?'

Sarah blushed scarlet. 'We are, as the film stars say, just good friends.'

'But he does go biking?'

'So what? Oh, I wish I could think of something really bitchy to say to you, Sister Croft!'

Sarah waltzed out, laughing, and Samantha looked at the two invitations in her hand—one for her and one for Bruce. Sarah had no idea where Laurie had gone, or even if he would make the party. She sighed, but couldn't decide if it was a sigh of relief or sadness. He was a glamorous glimpse into a world she could never again enter.

Grey skies and cool temperatures had given way to a patch of hot weather, and instead of putting away all her summer clothes Samantha now spent the rest of the day washing and pressing them, ready to wear.

The cream sundress that she had worn when she assisted Sir Ralph and Laurie in the operating theatre in Italy gave out a definite smell of antiseptic when immersed in warm water, and her pulse quickened. My hair had smelled the same, she recalled. I had to wash it in the shower once I returned to the villa.

I wore those shorts and that sun-top when Laurie made me laugh about Maria, and this pastel boob-tube when we lay on sunbeds and drowsed until the sun went in. Most of the garments were drip-dry, and she left them hanging over the bath for a while, ironing the ones that were not soiled but only creased.

Everything she wore had some memory of Amalfi and Laurie Martin, she found with growing dread. Will there ever be a time when I can wear them again without thinking of him? she thought.

She flung the linen hat he had found so amusing

into the back of her wardrobe and sat on the bed until she glanced at the clock and found she was due to meet Bruce in half an hour. Deliberately, she put on a summer dress that Laurie had eyed with such approval that she had been sure he must hear her heart beating, as the caress of his dark blue eyes had been almost a physical touch. She smoothed down the sleek short skirt and pulled the Lycra top down to make her cleavage show and her breasts jut proudly under the silky material. The sharp lime colour matched the stripe in her purple canvas loafers and she made up her lips with soft pinky brown colour.

There! An evening with Bruce might erase at least one memory, she decided, then she picked up her canvas bag and Bruce's invitation and walked quickly down the back stairs that led to the car park. A puff of cold air made her pause at the foot of the stairs, and she ran back to her room. The day had been hot, but the evening might get cool, and she had set out with no coat.

A man disappeard down the front stairs as she reached the corridor and she caught a glimpse of light cotton trousers and a bright blue shirt. There were two other small apartments on that level, used by house surgeons whom she had met at various times, but none of them had the height or the athletic build of the man who had now gone. Not every man in a blue shirt is Laurie Martin, she told herself sharply. Don't be neurotic! Someone had a visitor, that's all.

She found a short woollen jacket with well defined revers and big bronzy buttons, and almost ran down

the stairs again, thinking of nothing but the fact that
she might be late for her date, and she didn't see the
picture postcard that lay just inside the door.

'You look good enough to eat.' Bruce regarded
her with affection.

'I hope there's more on the menu than me,' she
replied, laughing. 'I'm hungry.'

'I wanted to book a table at the Elite, but I have
to see my patient later, so will you settle for the
Falcon?' He closed the door carefully and took his
own seat in the sober but expensive saloon car.
Briefly he touched her hand, then drove carefully
into the line of traffic leading up past the park gates
and on to the Falcon.

'Fine,' Samantha said, and fumbled in her hand-
bag. Her reaction to his touch had been a shock.
Not the same shock that she'd experienced when
Laurie took her hand, but the shock of knowing that
she felt no warm reaction whatever to the warm and
possessive contact that Bruce had made.

'Here we are,' he said with an air of discovery.

'Fine,' she said again, and handed him the invitation from Sarah. 'Before I forget to give it to you,'
she added. 'Sarah's handing out invitations as if they
were falling leaves. I hope she knows how many will
accept and has someone to stop gatecrashers.' I'm
waffling and I can feel a panic coming on, she
thought, and I don't want to be touched or kissed by
you, my dear, sweet man.

'Great. It should be quite an occasion.' Bruce
ordered drinks and they sat in the lounge until they
had chosen food from the menu and the waitress
told them their table was ready. 'I doubt if they'll

have gatecrashers at any party given by Sir Ralph,' he assured her.

'It is Sarah's party, and she has a lot of student friends,' she reminded him, thinking of Sarah dressed in black leather and the psychedelic crash helmet.

'She comes from a good family and I'm sure has been very well brought up,' he said with a hint of reproach.

'Sarah's a very nice girl,' Samantha agreed, 'but none of her crowd are what you might call conventional.' She looked at the smooth, good-looking face and wanted to ask, Where have you been all your life? but said nothing until he started talking about the standards of some of the medical students he had seen that day in the medical school.

'You were a student once,' she reminded him. 'Didn't you ever drink a little too much and make a row occasionally?'

'I was far too busy studying for my exams,' he said. 'I know a lot went on, but I kept a low profile and got where I wanted to be—one of the youngest consultant physicians the Royal Berks had ever produced, and now I have a practice in Harley Street and a very good life.'

'No moonlight swimming, no backpacking in Greece?' she asked in a teasing voice.

He replied seriously, 'Of course not. There wasn't time for that, but I have been to Greece and enjoyed it very much.' He named a famous tour operator that tailor-made visits to famous places in such a way that the traveller need never speak to a native of the country and could eat safe European food. His hand clasped hers. 'I'd like to take you there,' he said.

'I've been to the Islands,' Samantha told him with a smile. 'I got sunburned and had sand in my sleeping-bag.' She had a fleeting memory of Julian, the boy who died. 'Very gritty, the Greek sand, but the sunrise was wonderful.' She saw that Bruce wasn't amused. 'People change and their tastes change too,' she admitted. 'I confess that I did appreciate the luxury of Sir Ralph's villa in Amalfi as I was feeling limp after I lost my tonsils, and a sleeping-bag on a hard beach wouldn't have done anything for me!'

'I want to look after you,' Bruce said. 'When I saw how efficient you were that day in Theatre, and how calm and kind you were when I was clumsy, I decided then that you're the one person I want to share my life.'

Samantha gave his hand a reluctant squeeze and withdrew it from his grasp to sip her wine. 'We hardly know each other,' she protested weakly.

'Think about it, Samantha. I can give you a good life, and I'm not the sort to go after other women,' he added as if that was a ridiculous suggestion.

'I know. You're everything a sensible girl could want, Bruce, and I'm very fond of you, but. . .'

'No buts. I love you and I hope you'll marry me, but I know this is sudden. In fact, this is the most unpredictable decision I've ever made. Quite out of character, but I know I'm right. Think about it and we'll talk later.'

At the doorway to the block where she lived, Bruce kissed her twice and told her again that he

wanted to marry her. She smiled and drew away
gently, as she could think of no way that she wanted
to hurt him, but as she walked slowly up to her room
she was depressed.

What's wrong with me? she thought. Why can't I
take what many girls would grab with both hands—
to be the wife of a leading physician, to have every
luxury and care showered on me and the love of a
faithful and good man? At least he gave me time to
think, and maybe, once I've forgotten Laurie, I may
change my mind about a lot of things.

The picture postcard was crumpled where the
door had pushed it on to the carpet, and Samantha
bent to pick it up. She smoothed out the creases and
saw there was no stamp. She turned it over.

Remember me? Sarah invited me to her party and
expects us to go there together. Can you bear it?
I'll see you tomorrow. L.

Tears blurred the writing, and the scene of Amalfi
on the coloured side seemed drenched in rain.
'Leave me alone,' she whispered. 'Bruce wants to
marry me and care for me. Why don't you go back
to Caterina and never see me again?'

There were no cases for Sir Ralph the next day, and
Samantha got up early and went to the West End of
London for the day to avoid any possibility of seeing
Laurie, but as she sat in St James's Park, feeding the
ducks, she knew she couldn't avoid him for ever. He
would meet her in the theatre as soon as she started
her new job. Her troubles would never end so long

as she had to see him, perhaps touch him, and dream about his face.

There was only one answer. Marry Bruce and leave nursing for ever to run his home and maybe to produce well-brought-up children who might have similar ambitions to the ones Bruce had described. A sparrow landed on her outstretched hand and blinked at her, then flew away.

I can put off any decision, she decided. I'll fly away like you, little bird. Tomorrow Sir Ralph will do the last of his private cases and I'll be free to take leave until I sign on for my new job. It would mean missing the party, but Sarah would hardly notice the one small gap in her guest list.

I'll go to France for a couple of weeks, Samantha decided, knowing she had enough money for a simple touring holiday through Normandy. I can write to Bruce from there and let Beattie's know I can't take on the theatre job as I'm getting married. She gulped. This was the best solution.

Cautiously, as if Laurie or Bruce or both might be waiting for her in the building, Samantha walked softly up the back stairs and into her room, after an exhausting day in overheated shops, trying to kill time. A voice called her name to answer the phone, but she stayed with the light off in her room, and the caller must have given up, as no further call was made. Sir Ralph wanted to make an early start as he had cases elsewhere after going to another hospital to see patients.

'Must get organised for the party, and I've a lot of people to see,' he told her as he made the first incision at eight a.m. precisely. 'These ovaries were badly stuck down. I gave her time to recover from the ectopic pregnancy, but she isn't well, and this must be done now that she's strong enough to stay in Theatre until I've freed the adhesions.' The patient's own doctor scrubbed and the house surgeon assisted in what was a tedious but necessary procedure.

'Have we any amnion, Sister?' Sir Ralph asked at last, and his HS looked blank. Samantha opened the tiny envelope of amniotic membrane and handed it to him. 'Good girl. Not many people use it now, but in cases with such bad adhesions that might easily stick again a piece of this on a raw surface prevents that happening, and it becomes a part of the patient's own tissue. She might even manage a baby through the ovary and tube left. It looks much more healthy than I'd feared. We'll keep an eye on her.'

'I shan't see you again for a time, Sir Ralph,' Samantha said when they drank coffee together after the case. 'I've decided to go away again as I have two more weeks of leisure.'

'Good, but you'll scrub for all my NHS patients on your return,' he said with satisfaction. 'Have a good holiday, but don't stay away for too long. Got your ticket? Be sure to charge it to me.'

'Not yet.' Suddenly it was impossible to tell him she would never work for him again and that she was not going back to Amalfi.

'Go today. Don't waste time, but use the rest of your leave well, and enjoy life. I thought you looked a little bit depressed. Have I been working you too hard?'

'I've enjoyed it very much, but you're right—I need to get away again,' she agreed.

He laughed. 'And so you shall.' He picked up his heavy surgical bag and left her alone.

I can go, she decided. I can get to France by boat and then hire a car and wander down south. Or even go straight down to Toulon by train and hire a car there. She went to her room and began to pack. Twice she tried to ring the ferry company, but each time they seemed to be stacking calls, and she put down the receiver as another nurse wanted to use the phone. 'Sorry,' she explained. 'I'm trying to book a ticket.'

She tried again, and a pre-recorded message told her that the strike in French ports had disrupted ferries, and advised her to ring again tomorrow.

She packed and rang a travel agency. Maybe a flight would be better. The girl took her telephone number and promised to ring back if there was a place on any flight into northern France, but the ferry strike had made them busy.

Samantha made coffee and ate a slice of cake in her room, as she dared not go out for food in case the telephone rang, and when it did she heard someone answer it and decided that the call wasn't for her but for the nurse who had been hovering close to the phone for an hour.

'Nurse Croft?' She opened her door. 'Message for you. There's a ticket waiting for you at the airport. Enquire at the desk, and be there by two this afternoon if you want it.' She named the airline and sighed. 'Lucky old you. I'm not due for a holiday for another three months and Men's Medical is really bad just now.'

'Is that all she said?' Samantha gave a nervous

laugh. 'This might be a mystery tour, as I asked for any flight to anywhere in northern France.' She shrugged. 'Well, live dangerously, I suppose!'

'It was a man's voice, and he was in a tearing hurry and asked me to leave the message for you as I said I knew you were in your room.'

Samantha locked her cupboard and made sure she had her passport and credit cards and cheque-book. She checked the time and knew that if she wanted to be at the airport in time to pick up her ticket and put her luggage through the check-in she had to hurry.

The taxi seemed to attract red lights, but at last Samantha stumbled on to the train to the airport with a sigh of relief. The huge reception area was daunting, but she saw a notice marked 'Enquiries' and made for it. She was directed to the airline desk and told the clerk her name.

'Check in over there, and your flight is on time, gate twenty-four. Just half an hour to wait.'

'Who do I see to pay for my ticket?' she asked.

'Not me,' he shrugged. 'Your ticket is in order and you have a non-smoking club class seat. Get in touch with the travel agency when you get back,' he advised. 'The ticket was handed in for you to collect.'

'Club class?' she said, but he was already dealing with another enquiry. Well, she hadn't specified which class she wanted, and it was a late booking, so she would have to live it up a little for once. She examined the ticket more closely and gasped. She checked the flight number and looked at the video display, and they matched. The ticket was for Italy, not France.

'Come on,' a deep familiar voice said, 'let's get through Passport Control and I'll buy you some coffee.'

'Laurie!' she gasped. 'What are you doing here?'

'The same as you. Ralph told me he'd booked a ticket for me today, and here I am.' He grinned. 'He said I'd have company, and to take care of you, as you were his guest.' He eyed her stricken face with a solemn expression, but his eyes sparkled deep blue, as deep as the Bay of Amalfi. 'A very ruthless man, our favourite consultant,' he said. 'Tell me, where were you really heading for? The nurse on the phone said you were expecting a call from a travel agency.'

'France,' Samantha said in a small voice. 'I don't want to go to Italy.'

'No?' He took her flight bag as if she might run away if he didn't hold her prisoner. 'We can go there another time.'

The line of passengers built up behind them, and Samantha found herself carried along with them. She glanced at the wonderful face and the strong broad shoulders, and she wanted him as she had never wanted anything or anyone in her life.

She sat where she was put and ate what was put before her, tasting nothing and only sipping the wine, and found it impossible to make coherent conversation with the man she now knew could never be banished from her thoughts and her heart.

Laurie talked about Sir Ralph and Guido and Carol, and gently made her respond and talk about her future at Beattie's. He reached over to put her table back after the meal was finished, and his hand touched her wrist, then engulfed her own hand in a tender grasp. She tried to think that this man was playing with her emotions, that Caterina was the love of his life who would never let him go, and she couldn't meet the love that shone from his eyes as he caressed her hand.

'Someone asked me to marry him,' she blurted out at last when the tension grew to screaming-point.

'I know,' he answered calmly. 'I met him last night when we checked our patient, and I'm afraid he's going to be a very disappointed man when you tell him your answer.'

'What makes you think I shall refuse him?'

'You don't love him.'

'Is everything all right?' The stewardess checked that their seatbelts were fixed, ready for landing.

'Fine,' Laurie said. 'What's the weather like in Naples?'

'Hot and getting hotter,' the girl said. 'The coast is sizzling.'

'What a good thing we're going up to the mountains,' Laurie said with a smile at Samantha.

'The mountains? I thought we were going to the villa?'

'And have Maria fussing over us, and having to spend all day in the pool to keep fairly cool in this heat?'

'Then where?' she asked.

'Didn't I tell you? I've bought a chalet in the hills. We can still see the ocean and have plenty of sun, but it's fresh and cool up there at night, and often we shall need log fires. Come on, we can go now.' They disembarked and he strode along to the luggage retrieval, and soon they were bundling their luggage into the trunk of a hire car.

Samantha hung back. 'You can't just make me go there with you. Sir Ralph told me I could stay at the villa, so will you please take me there?' she said firmly. She knew how it would be. Away from the eyes of his friends and the constant presence of Maria, Laurie could do as he liked with her. He wanted her with a passion that she could sense each time he looked at her, but if she once gave in to him her life would be ruined. The old word enthralled had meant to be in a person's power, and that was how it would be for her, for ever, even if he cast her aside once he had slaked his lust and gone back to being the slave of Caterina.

'I've put in too much work on this to stop now,' he told her. 'It's all arranged, and they'll be waiting for us.'

'Who's waiting?' she queried.

'Not now—tomorrow morning. You did bring it with you, I hope?'

'Bring what?' she asked weakly. 'Have I missed a message or two, or a hundred?'

'I don't mean that awful sunhat,' he said with gentle irony. 'I mean the dress from Positano.' She nodded. 'Good. We'll ask the maid at the hotel to press it tonight ready for the morning.'

'Hotel?' she echoed.

'You really mustn't repeat everything I say, darling. We stay at a hotel tonight and meet Guido and the others tomorrow.'

'Why? Is there another festival?'

'The greatest one on earth. Here we are, and

there's Guido to greet us, cold sober and very smart,' Laurie added with a laugh as he waved to the man in the bright orange shirt and blue shorts which came under his paunch.

Guido seized her hand and a flood of incomprehensible Italian flowed from his mouth.

'Hello, it's good to see you again,' Samantha said politely.

'He said everything is under control. We stay here tonight, and then I think we can look forward to two whole weeks away from everyone. Just one small matter to check.' Laurie spoke to Guido, who produced a velvet-covered box and led the way into the hotel lounge, where he put the box on a table and Laurie opened it. Samantha gasped. Inside were six gold rings, three slender and smaller than the other broad, heavy rings worn by continental men.

'Try them for size,' he said, and put one on his finger. Guido took Samantha's nerveless hand and tried on the rings. One fitted perfectly, and she gazed at it in disbelief, then burst into tears.

'You're cruel,' she whispered. 'You're in love with Caterina and yet you try to use me. I suppose you want to make people think we're man and wife when you get me to that hidden love-nest in the hills! Well, you'll be disappointed. I hate you, Laurie Martin, and I'm going to get a taxi to take me to the villa!'

'*Bella, bella,*' Guido said as her cheeks burned and her eyes flashed fire. 'There must be Italian blood somewhere!' He picked up the rings after putting a small marker on the ones that had fitted, and shrugged. 'Women weep at anything. My wife cried for hours before our wedding. See you in church,' he added.

'Church?' Surely he was trying to be macho-American, using a slang phrase, but Laurie took her by the arm and led her to follow the porter to the elevator.

'Church. Not a cathedral, but a simple village church, and you shall wear the dress you bought here.' He spoke in a low voice, firmly but with a slight tremor. 'You will marry me, Samantha?'

She looked at the bored face of the porter in the elevator with them and a hysterical laugh began to surface. The lift sighed and stopped, and the porter produced two keys and unlocked the first room.

The single room overlooked the garden, a terrace of tumbling, untidy vines, unlike any she had seen in France in regimented rows. The porter was dismissed to open the second room, and Laurie took her into his arms. 'Carol told me you thought I was in love with Caterina and I knew I could explain, but Bruce seemed so certain you'd marry him that I had to act fast.'

Her body tensed. 'You haven't explained,' she said. 'You went after her even when she was married.'

'When a woman is so tormented with guilt that she threatens suicide, what would you do? I persuaded her to tell Paolo the truth and she found he already knew!'

'It made no difference? I thought Italian men liked their brides to be pure.'

'He wanted her above all women, as I want you. Now will you believe me?' Laurie kissed her wet eyelids and her now pale cheeks, and his questing lips found the trembling corners of her mouth as her arms ventured to hold him and her hand caressed the mane of dark hair.

Her body seemed to melt and blend with his hard thighs and her breasts thrust against him, longing to be caressed, kissed and brought to agonising rapture, but he put her away from him. His eyes were wild with desire and he was breathless.

'Tomorrow,' he said. 'Why do you think I avoided you before I knew you loved me? I couldn't bear to touch you as I was on fire, even in the theatre when I could see only your eyes.'

'And now?' Samantha's eyes felt heavy-lidded and her body strange and alluring, and she felt as reckless as the undisciplined vines. 'You booked separate rooms?'

'It's usual before a wedding.'

'What a waste, but we can rumple up the sheets.' She was calm now with the vision of life stretching into a golden future wherever he wanted to take her, wherever fate sent them together.

With a soft moan she sank back on the bed and watched him slip out of his clothes. In hospital, she had seen naked men, but never like this. He unbuttoned her shirt and let his hand rest on her breast. She closed her eyes as his kisses came long and hard, and his body came down at last, when she almost pleaded for mercy, to make a union that sent tears gushing from her eyes and brought a wonderful peace to her heart.

— MEDICAL ♥ ROMANCE —

The books for enjoyment this month are:

SURGEON OF THE HEART Sharon Wirdnam
A GENTLE GIANT Caroline Anderson
DREAM OF NAPLES Lisa Cooper
HAND IN HAND Margaret Barker

♥ ♥ ♥ ♥ ♥

Treats In store!

Watch next month for the following absorbing stories:

GYPSY SUMMER Laura MacDonald
THE BECKHILL TRADITION Lilian Darcy
THE DOCTORS AT SEFTONBRIDGE Janet Ferguson
A MIDWIFE'S CHOICE Margaret Holt